A FEAST OF THORNS AND ROSES

A
FEAST
OF
THORNS
AND ROSES

THE UNOFFICIAL COOKBOOK OF
A COURT OF THORNS AND ROSES

CHELSEA COLE

weldon**owen**

For Reggie

Born as this journey began,
and my greatest adventure yet.

CONTENTS

Note from the Author

Dear Fellow ACOTAR Fans,

Welcome to *A Feast of Thorns and Roses*, a culinary journey inspired by the world of Sarah J. Maas's A Court of Thorns and Roses series. I am thrilled to share this collection of recipes with you, each one a tribute to the vivid universe that Maas has woven together—a world with which, like many of you, I have fallen in love.

For years, I'd been searching for a story that could reignite the sense of wonder I'd often felt in my early years of reading. When I stumbled upon *A Court of Thorns and Roses*, it was as if I'd walked through a secret door into a world of enchantment, danger, love, and resilience. The way Maas crafted Feyre and her journey is magical, but beyond the plot and characters, what truly resonated with me was how Maas used food to help her paint her vivid scenes.

Throughout the series, meals are more than simply sustenance; they are expressions of culture, emotion, and connection. Whether it's a hearty breakfast before a day of rigorous training, a snack while hiking through the wilderness, a cozy dinner among friends, or a lavish feast in a grand dining hall, each meal adds depth and color to her storytelling. I found myself inspired to recreate these meals in my own kitchen. This cookbook is my attempt to bring those moments to your table, to let you feel the warmth of a simple meal shared in the cozy confines of a dinner with the Inner Circle or taste the richness of the Winter Solstice feast.

In *A Feast of Thorns and Roses*, you'll find recipes for exact dishes described in the books as well

as creations inspired by beloved characters, the ambience of the courts, and the spirit of places such as Adriata and the Rainbow Quarter. From the rich flavors of the Night Court to the fresh dishes of the Spring Court, I crafted each recipe to transport you into the world of Prythian, allowing you to experience the magic of the story in a new, delicious way.

Creating this cookbook has been unlike any other project I've worked on. I've been food blogging for over a decade and written two other cookbooks, but I've done nothing as creative and, frankly, as fun as this! As I dreamt up recipes and experimented with flavors, I found myself diving deeper into the series, exploring the qualities that make each court unique, and learning about the characters more intimately through the foods they might enjoy. It was a process that not only challenged my culinary skills but also deepened my appreciation for the intricate world that Maas has created.

Whether you're a seasoned cook or a novice in the kitchen, my goal is that this cookbook offers you an opportunity to bring these beloved books to life in a new way. I hope you enjoy preparing these dishes as much as you've enjoyed journeying with Feyre through Prythian. Gather your friends and family or make a spread all for yourself—after all, every meal is a celebration in the world of ACOTAR.

Until the stars listen and dreams are answered,

Chelsea Cole

How to Use this Book

This cookbook is designed to bring the flavors of Prythian into your kitchen and make the magic of Sarah J. Maas's stories come alive through food. Whether you're a seasoned cook or let's just say, a reluctant chef, these recipes are written to be approachable and delicious.

ORGANIZATION

The book follows a traditional structure, starting with breakfast recipes and progressing through appetizers, mains, sides, desserts, and cocktails. You'll find two dessert sections: one featuring grand desserts inspired by each of the courts in the series, and another with simpler, snackable treats drawn from memorable book moments. The cocktail section has a signature drink for each member of the Inner Circle and the Archeron sisters. Each recipe section is intended to be flexible, allowing you to either follow the book in order or skip around to whatever seems yummy.

SHORTCUTS

These recipes are designed to be accessible for any home cook. Feel free to make them your own—if you spot a shortcut that suits your style, like using a boxed cake mix, go for it! My goal is to make cooking these recipes fun and easy to prepare, not a test of your culinary skills.

INGREDIENTS

You won't need to go on a grocery store scavenger hunt when using these books; all recipes are created with accessibility in mind. For instance, while the original books might mention rabbit or venison, we stick to more readily available options like chicken or beef. There are a couple exceptions to this rule, but that's made clear in their titles, and it's up to you whether or not you'd like to tackle them! When it comes to salt, I've used kosher salt for all the recipes—Diamond Crystal is my go-to. If you use a different type of salt, you may want to adjust the amount called for.

EQUIPMENT

To make the recipes in this book, you likely already have everything you'll need. Here are the pieces of equipment I recommend having on hand—they'll do you well beyond this cookbook!

* A stand mixer is handy but not essential; a good hand mixer can do the job just as well.
* A fine mesh strainer
* Muffin pans
* Mini muffin pans
* Rimmed baking sheets
* Wire cooling racks
* A Dutch oven
* A 3-tablespoon scoop (like an ice cream scoop)

ADVICE FROM ALIS

Keep an eye out for the sections called "Advice from Alis." These are tips and tricks from our favorite Spring Court maid tailored to each recipe. Her insights will help you navigate tricky steps or add a special touch to your dishes.

MENUS AND PARTIES

This cookbook isn't just a collection of recipes; it's an invitation to celebrate the world of ACOTAR. At the end of the book, you'll find menu suggestions for themed parties and gatherings. Whether you're hosting a small get-together or a large feast, these ideas will help you plan an event that feels like it's straight out of the books.

ENJOYING THE COOKBOOK

Above all, this book is a tribute to a series that has captivated so many of us. I hope you find it a handy resource in your kitchen, a source of inspiration for your gatherings, and a new way to connect with the beloved world of ACOTAR. Here's to many magical meals and memorable moments!

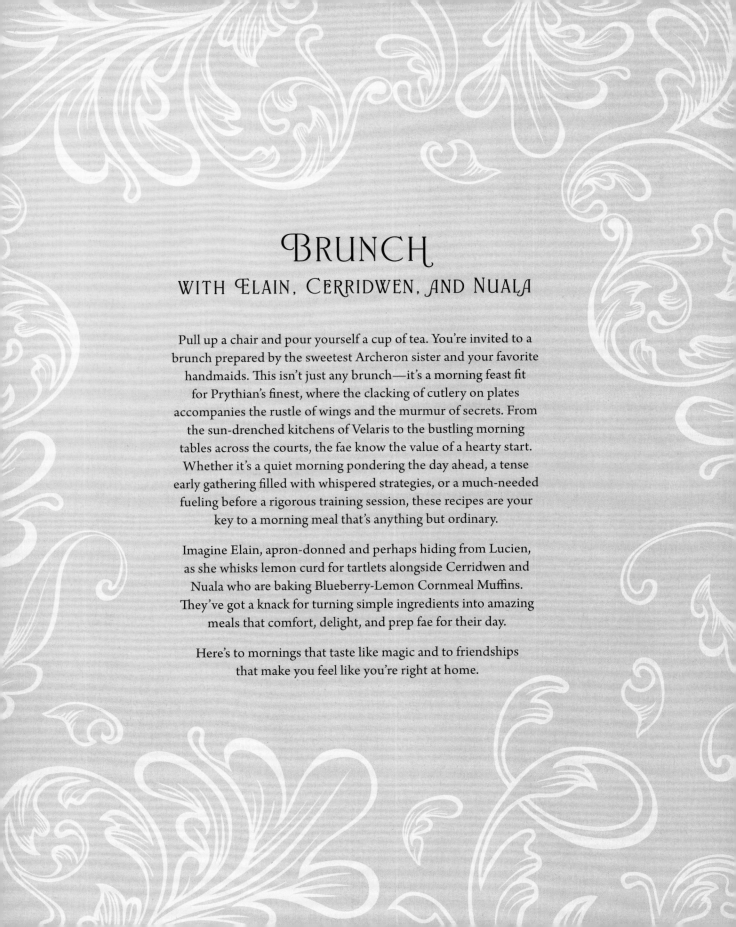

Brunch
with Elain, Cerridwen, and Nuala

Pull up a chair and pour yourself a cup of tea. You're invited to a brunch prepared by the sweetest Archeron sister and your favorite handmaids. This isn't just any brunch—it's a morning feast fit for Prythian's finest, where the clacking of cutlery on plates accompanies the rustle of wings and the murmur of secrets. From the sun-drenched kitchens of Velaris to the bustling morning tables across the courts, the fae know the value of a hearty start. Whether it's a quiet morning pondering the day ahead, a tense early gathering filled with whispered strategies, or a much-needed fueling before a rigorous training session, these recipes are your key to a morning meal that's anything but ordinary.

Imagine Elain, apron-donned and perhaps hiding from Lucien, as she whisks lemon curd for tartlets alongside Cerridwen and Nuala who are baking Blueberry-Lemon Cornmeal Muffins. They've got a knack for turning simple ingredients into amazing meals that comfort, delight, and prep fae for their day.

Here's to mornings that taste like magic and to friendships that make you feel like you're right at home.

Lemon Curd
Tartlets

YIELDS
12
TARTLETS

While the Spring Court lights up with Calanmai's wild festivities, Feyre's in the kitchen turning lemons into tartlets—not quite the magic you'd expect on Fire Night, but hey, it's something. As Tamlin does his duty as High Lord, and Feyre decides if she can't join the magic making, she'll at least indulge in a few treats, like a tiny lemon tart. These are perfect for munching while you're moping when you need a zesty pick-me-up. So, let's get baking—because if Feyre has to suffer through Calanmai wondering what Tamlin is doing, you bet she's going to do it with a delicious tartlet in hand.

1 package prepared, unbaked piecrusts (2 crusts)

FOR THE LEMON CURD

2 tablespoons finely grated lemon zest (from about 2 lemons)

¾ cup fresh lemon juice (from 2 to 3 lemons)

1¼ cups sugar

1¼ cups (2½ sticks) unsalted butter

5 large eggs

5 large egg yolks

FOR THE DECORATION (OPTIONAL)

Thinly cut lemon slices

Prepared whipped cream

Preheat the oven to 425°F.

Arrange the piecrusts on a work surface. Using a biscuit cutter or simply a wide-mouthed glass or jar, cut the piecrusts into twelve 4-inch circles. Discard any dough scraps or save for another use, if desired. Push 1 dough circle evenly into each prepared muffin cup. Prick the bottoms with a fork. Pre-bake in the preheated oven for 10 minutes, then set aside to cool.

Reduce the oven temperature to 350°F.

To make the lemon curd, in a saucepan over medium-low heat, whisk together the lemon zest, lemon juice, sugar, butter, eggs, and egg yolks. Continuously whisk until the butter melts and the mixture thickens enough to briefly hold its shape on the surface when dolloped, about 5 minutes.

Strain the hot lemon curd through a fine mesh strainer into a heat-safe bowl to remove any clumps and the zest.

Divide the lemon curd evenly among the pre-baked piecrusts, smoothing the surface with a spatula. Bake until the curd is thick and jiggles rather than "sloshes" when shaking the pan, about 5 minutes. The curd will still be soft but will set more as it cools.

Allow the tartlets to cool in the muffin pan for 30 minutes, then remove to a plate, cover with plastic wrap, and chill in the refrigerator for at least 1 hour or up to 3 days.

If desired, decorate with thinly sliced lemons and serve with whipped cream.

ADVICE FROM ALIS
You might stumble upon mini pie shells at the market. If you're fortunate enough to spot them, go ahead and grab 'em. They'll make this recipe even simpler, I reckon! Simply disregard the piecrust directions here, and heed the instructions on the package for any pre-baking, Dear.

BAKED
APPLE PORRIDGE
WITH SPICED PECANS

Porridge, a staple at many breakfasts across Prythian, provides a hearty start to the day, much like the bowl set before Feyre on her first morning at the Spring Court (although we'll pass on the anger rolling across the table from Lucien). This baked version makes the dish even simpler to prepare ahead of time. Tart apples and crunchy spiced pecans take this classically comforting dish to the next level, and you'll find it's perfect for sharing.

FOR THE SPICED PECANS

1 large egg white, lightly beaten

1 tablespoon water

3 cups pecan pieces

½ cup sugar

1 teaspoon ground cinnamon

½ teaspoon salt

½ teaspoon ground cloves

½ teaspoon ground nutmeg

FOR THE BAKED PORRIDGE

Nonstick cooking spray

1¾ cups milk (any type)

2 large eggs

½ cup pure maple syrup

¼ cup (½ stick) unsalted butter, melted and slightly cooled

¼ cup unsweetened applesauce

3 cups old-fashioned rolled oats

1 teaspoon baking powder

1 teaspoon ground cinnamon

1 teaspoon pure vanilla extract

¼ teaspoon salt

1½ cups peeled, cored, and diced Granny Smith apples (about 2 medium apples)

Preheat the oven to 350ºF. Line a baking sheet with aluminum foil.

To make the Spiced Pecans, beat the egg white and water together in a large bowl. Add the pecans and stir to coat. Mix the sugar, cinnamon, salt, cloves, and nutmeg in a small bowl; sprinkle over the moistened nuts and stir to coat.

Spread the coated nuts on the prepared pan. Bake in the preheated oven, stirring once halfway through, until toasted and fragrant, about 30 minutes. Set aside to cool.

To make the Baked Porridge, spray a 9-by-9-inch baking pan with nonstick cooking spray.

In a large bowl, whisk together the milk, eggs, syrup, melted butter, and applesauce. Stir in the oats, baking powder, cinnamon, vanilla extract, and salt until well mixed. Stir in the apples until evenly distributed.

Pour the oat-apple mixture into the prepared baking pan. Bake until the center appears almost set, but still slightly soft, about 35 minutes.

Remove from the oven and let cool for 5 minutes before serving. Spoon or slice and transfer to bowls. Top with the spiced pecans.

QUICHE WITH GOUDA, BACON, AND LEEKS

Channeling a frosty family meet-up in the human lands, this quiche is anything but. Loaded with crispy bacon, mild leeks, and gooey cheese, it's a dish that could make anyone forget about the awkwardness of bringing your new Fae friends to meet your iron-wearing human sisters. It's the perfect, comforting breakfast casserole to pass around—even when the conversation is as prickly as a thorn bush.

1 prepared, unbaked refrigerated or frozen deep-dish piecrust

6 large eggs

½ cup milk (any type)

¼ cup heavy cream

½ teaspoon salt

¼ teaspoon black pepper

6 slices bacon, cooked until crisp and crumbled

1½ cups chopped leeks (white and light green parts only), rinsed well

4 ounces Gouda cheese, cut into cubes

Preheat the oven to 375°F. If the piecrust comes in its own baking pan, set it aside on a work surface. If the piecrust comes folded, transfer it to a 9-inch regular or deep-dish pie pan and flute or crimp the edges as desired; set aside on a work surface.

In a large bowl, whisk together the eggs, milk, heavy cream, salt, and pepper until well blended.

Sprinkle the crumbled bacon, chopped leeks, and cubed Gouda cheese evenly onto the bottom of the piecrust. Pour the egg mixture over the bacon, leeks, and cheese in the piecrust.

Bake in the preheated oven until the center is completely set and the top is golden brown, 30 to 35 minutes.

Remove the quiche from the oven and let cool for 5 to 10 minutes before slicing into 8 wedges.

Serve warm or let cool completely, cover with plastic wrap, and refrigerate for up to 3 days before reheating and serving.

If making in advance, reheat the quiche in the oven at 375°F for 15 to 20 minutes before serving.

ADVICE FROM ALIS

This quiche preserves its charm even when frozen. Why not double the recipe and prepare an extra to enjoy later? Once it's cooked and cooled, enfold the quiche in foil, nestle it into a plastic bag safe for the freezer, and let it sleep in the frost. To warm it anew, thaw it in the refrigerator over the night and then warm it as instructed, Love.

THE SURIEL'S
ALMOND TEA CAKES

Ready to listen to the most knowledgeable creature in Prythian "spill the tea"? These almond tea cakes are a tribute to The Suriel, a being bound to reveal truths to those who catch it. While catching The Suriel might be a daunting task, catching up with friends over these delightful blueberry-spiked tea cakes is easy. Perfectly golden with a delicate crumb, these cakes are infused with a subtle sweetness of honey and tart fruit, making every bite a delicious blend of flavors. Enjoy with tea or coffee, as desired.

Nonstick cooking spray, for greasing

¾ cup (1½ sticks) cold unsalted butter

1⅓ cups almond flour

½ cup all-purpose flour

1¾ cups powdered sugar, plus extra for dusting

½ teaspoon kosher salt

5 large egg whites, at room temperature

2 tablespoons honey

1 teaspoon pure almond extract

1 cup fresh or frozen blueberries

Preheat the oven to 350ºF. Lightly grease the cups of two 24-cup mini-muffin pans with cooking spray.

In a saucepan over medium heat, melt the butter. Swirl the butter in the pan and continue to cook, swirling the pan occasionally, until it turns golden and smells nutty, about 5 minutes. Pour the browned butter into a heat-safe bowl and allow it to cool to room temperature.

In a large bowl, combine the almond flour, all-purpose flour, powdered sugar, and salt.

Stir in the egg whites, honey, almond extract, and cooled browned butter until well mixed.

Scoop 1 tablespoon of batter into each prepared muffin cup. Top each with 1 or 2 blueberries.

Bake the cakes until golden brown around the edges and firm to the touch in the center, 15 to 18 minutes.

Remove the cakes from the oven and allow them to cool in the pan for 5 minutes. Then, transfer them to a wire rack to cool completely.

Once cooled, dust the tea cakes with powdered sugar before serving.

ADVICE FROM ALIS
Don't hesitate to exchange the blueberries for a different berry, or perhaps a dollop of jam, if it pleases you, Love.

CHEESE AND CHIVE SCONES

In the mist-shrouded first few mornings at the Night Court, Feyre finds solace in the comforting dishes baked by Nuala and Cerridwen. These scones, enjoyed in a moment of reflection after (unknowingly) helping Rhys capture an Attor, become a quiet respite as Feyre navigates the looming threat of war with Hybern. With savory notes of sharp Cheddar and the freshness of chives, these scones are perfect whether you're enjoying brunch with friends or contemplating the complexities of your new life in Prythian.

2½ cups all-purpose flour

2 teaspoons baking powder

1 teaspoon baking soda

1 teaspoon sugar

½ teaspoon salt

¼ teaspoon cayenne pepper

⅓ cup cold salted butter, cut into ½-inch cubes

1½ cups shredded Cheddar cheese

2 tablespoons chopped fresh chives

2 large eggs

Scant 1 cup heavy cream

Preheat the oven to 400°F.

In a large bowl, combine the flour, baking powder, baking soda, sugar, salt, and cayenne pepper. Add the cubes and toss to coat. Using a fork or your fingers, press the mixture until the butter is well incorporated and it becomes crumbly. Stir in the Cheddar cheese and chives until evenly combined.

In a separate bowl, whisk together the eggs and heavy cream. Add the egg-cream mixture to the flour mixture, stirring just until a dough forms. The mixture will be somewhat dry.

Use your hands to knead the dough gently on a lightly floured surface, just until it comes together. Form the dough into an 8-inch disk. Using a sharp knife, cut the disk into 8 wedges, as if cutting a pizza. Place the wedges about 1 inch apart on an ungreased baking sheet.

Bake the scones in the preheated oven until golden brown, 15 to 18 minutes. Allow the scones to cool on the baking sheet for 5 minutes before serving.

ADVICE FROM ALIS

These scones make a delightful addition to a brunch spread or as a companion to the various soup recipes nestled within the pages of this book. They're most enchanting when warm, though they hold their charm even when left to greet the room's air, Love.

BLUEBERRY–LEMON
CORNMEAL MUFFINS

Start your morning like you're seated at the breakfast table in the Night Court, where there always seems to be a platter of muffins. These muffins are studded with bursts of blueberries, a hint of lemon zest, and crunchy cornmeal for a delicate sweetness and texture. Whether you're sharing breakfast with a conversational sparring partner like Rhys or simply enjoying the quietude of dawn, these muffins are perfect accompanied by a steaming cup of tea or coffee.

2 cups all-purpose flour

½ cup cornmeal

1½ teaspoons baking powder

½ teaspoon kosher salt

2 cups fresh or frozen blueberries

1 cup sugar

½ cup (1 stick) unsalted butter, at room temperature

Finely grated zest of 1 large lemon

½ cup milk (any type)

ADVICE FROM ALIS
Thinking of forgoing the cornmeal, Dear? You might fancy almond flour for a touch of nuttiness, or just use all-purpose flour in its stead.

Preheat the oven to 350°F. Line a 12-cup muffin pan with paper liners.

In a large bowl, whisk together the flour, cornmeal, baking powder, and salt. In a separate bowl, toss the blueberries with ¼ cup of the flour mixture to coat. This helps prevent the blueberries from sinking during baking.

In the bowl of a stand mixer fitted with the paddle attachment, cream together the sugar, butter, and lemon zest until the mixture is light and fluffy, about 3 minutes. With the mixer on low speed, gradually pour in the milk until just blended. Continuing on low speed, slowly add the flour mixture, adding it about ½ cup at a time, until just incorporated. Do not overmix. Stop the mixture and gently fold in the blueberries using a rubber spatula.

Using a 3-tablespoon scoop, distribute the batter evenly among the prepared muffin cups, filling each about two-thirds full (about 2 scoops each).

Bake the muffins until the tops are golden brown and a toothpick inserted into the center of a muffin comes out clean, 15 to 18 minutes.

Allow the muffins to cool in the pan for 5 minutes, then transfer them to a wire rack to cool for an additional 10 to 15 minutes before serving.

STARTERS
IN THE SPRING COURT

The Spring Court is a realm of beauty shadowed by turmoil. The recipes in this section capture the essence of a land that Feyre first knew as a haven, a place of blossoming love and dazzling magic nestled among rolling green hills and lush forests. Yet, as the series unfolds, this paradise reveals its thorns, from Tamlin's descent into obsession to the fraying at the seams of the Court, mirroring the manor at its heart—once a symbol of grandeur, now a testament to neglect.

Through dishes such as Deviled Eggs with Bacon Roses and Thyme Thorns and Upside-Down Onion Parmesan Tarts, we pay homage to the court's dual nature. These starters, with their blend of vibrant flavors and textures, are a nod to the Spring Court's complexity—from its intoxicating beauty to its underlying darkness.

This collection of recipes invites you to taste the Spring Court's layered stories, where every bite holds the echo of Feyre's journey: from love's first bloom to the courage to confront one's own thorns. Let these dishes be a tribute to the resilience found amidst the ruins.

Deviled Eggs with Bacon Roses and Thyme Thorns

YIELDS

8

SERVINGS

For a taste of the Spring Court, whip up these classic deviled eggs with a special addition: bacon roses and thyme thorns. These are perfect for when you want to add a bit of Tamlin's regality to your table—without the drama. They have all his flavor and just a bit of his fierceness thanks to the horseradish cream. These crowd-pleasing deviled eggs are the perfect way to bring some Spring Court elegance to your table. Like Tamlin himself, deviled eggs are always delicious . . . until you've had too much.

8 slices bacon

8 large eggs, hard-boiled, peeled, and halved

¼ cup mayonnaise

1 tablespoon Dijon mustard

1 tablespoon prepared horseradish

1 tablespoon chopped fresh dill

½ teaspoon kosher salt

¼ teaspoon freshly ground black pepper

¼ teaspoon garlic powder

Thyme sprigs, for garnish

Preheat the oven to 375ºF. Line a rimmed baking sheet with foil and place a wire rack over the top.

Cut the bacon slices in half lengthwise to create thinner strips. Starting at one end of a bacon strip, roll it up tightly to form a rosette, leaving about 3 inches unrolled. Twist the remaining unrolled part and continue to roll it around the rosette, securing it with a toothpick. Place it on the wire rack. Repeat with the remaining bacon strips. Bake the bacon rosettes in the preheated oven until crisp, 40 to 45 minutes. Set aside to cool.

Remove the yolks from the egg halves and transfer to a bowl. Add the mayonnaise, mustard, horseradish, dill, salt, black pepper, and garlic powder. Mash and stir together with a fork until smooth.

Arrange the egg white halves on a plate, cavity side up. Transfer the yolk mixture to a gallon-sized zipper-top bag. Cut off one corner of the bag to create a small hole. Press the yolk mixture through the hole into the egg white halves, dividing it evenly. Cut the thyme sprigs into ½ inch pieces and place two pieces on each egg half. Top each with a bacon rose. Refrigerate the deviled eggs until ready to serve.

MELON CAPRESE WITH LEMON BASIL VINAIGRETTE

Is it even breakfast in Prythian if melons aren't on the table? Sweet, ripe melons pair perfectly with creamy mozzarella pearls, and the zesty, lemon-basil vinaigrette makes for a refreshing combination that'll transport you to a sunlit dining room in any of the Court's manors. Keep things vegetarian or give this salad a salty kick with the addition of crispy prosciutto.

FOR THE SALAD

½ *ripe cantaloupe*

½ *ripe honeydew melon*

½ *ripe small watermelon*

One 8-ounce package mozzarella pearls (not marinated), drained

FOR THE VINAIGRETTE

¼ *cup packed fresh basil leaves*

Juice of 1 lemon (about 2 tablespoons)

2 tablespoons extra-virgin olive oil

1 tablespoon honey, plus more if needed

¼ *teaspoon kosher salt*

4 slices prosciutto (optional)

To make the salad, use a melon baller to scoop small balls from the cantaloupe, honeydew, and watermelon halves. Alternatively, dice each of the melons into 1-inch pieces, discarding the rind. Place the melon balls or pieces into a large bowl. Add the mozzarella pearls.

To make the vinaigrette, combine the basil leaves, lemon juice, olive oil, honey, and salt in a blender or food processor. Blend until smooth. Taste and adjust with additional honey if desired.

Pour the vinaigrette over the melon and mozzarella mixture. Toss gently to coat all the ingredients evenly.

Serve the salad immediately, or for added crunch, garnish with crispy prosciutto: Pan-fry the prosciutto slices until crispy, then tear into bite-sized pieces and sprinkle over the salad before serving.

SIMPLE
LEMONY GREEN SALAD

In the Spring Court, even salads get a dash of drama. Picture a blend of the freshest greens and herbs from Tamlin's own gardens, spruced up with a zingy lemon–olive oil dressing. This starter or side dish is your quick fix to adding a bright, light-hearted touch to any spread. It's perfect for those days when you crave a slice of spring without the fuss. Whip it up fast, serve it with a smirk, and watch it disappear more quickly than Feyre's patience with Tamlin.

5 cups mixed spring greens

¼ cup chopped fresh flat leaf parsley

2 tablespoons chopped fresh dill

2 tablespoons chopped fresh basil

Juice of ½ lemon (about 1 tablespoon)

1 tablespoon extra-virgin olive oil

½ teaspoon flaky sea salt, such as Maldon

In a large bowl, toss together the spring greens, parsley, dill, and basil.

Squeeze the lemon juice over the greens and drizzle with olive oil. Sprinkle the flaky sea salt over the top and toss to coat evenly.

Serve immediately.

OYSTERS ON THE HALF SHELL WITH SPICY MIGNONETTE

With this appetizer, we're departing from the rolling hills of spring and saying hello to the Summer Court. Indulge in Adriata's bounty with oysters on the half shell, complemented by a spicy mignonette, something that would be sure to be served at Tarquin's vibrant and welcoming court. As you savor this briny nod to the Summer Court's oceanic fare, picture yourself above a sun-drenched beach with the gentle sea breeze carrying the laughter of courtiers, overlooking the turquoise Adriatic seas with red-roofed buildings in the background.

¼ cup minced shallots

2 tablespoons minced jalapeño

¼ cup red wine vinegar

½ teaspoon sugar

¼ teaspoon kosher salt

¼ teaspoon freshly cracked black pepper

Crushed ice, for serving

Two dozen fresh raw oysters, shucked, juices reserved

In a small bowl, mix together the shallots, jalapeño, red wine vinegar, sugar, salt, and black pepper to create the mignonette.

Scatter crushed ice over a large, rimmed platter. Arrange the oysters on the ice, taking care not to spill the juices. Top each oyster with about one teaspoon of the mignonette. Add the remaining mignonette to a small serving bowl with a spoon to serve on the side. Serve right away.

ADVICE FROM ALIS

Oysters can be found at many a grocer, but for the freshest bounty, best befriend your local fishmonger—who may even take to shucking them for you, Love.

Upside-Down
Onion Parmesan Tarts

Indulge in an appetizer that embodies the court's duality of elegance and earthiness. Whether amidst the blooming gardens of Tamlin's estate or in a quaint village near its borders, this treat bridges the gap between the opulent feasts of the Fae and the homely comfort of the human realm. Flaky puff pastry topped with a melty mixture of onions, honey, and nutty Parmesan, these tartlets are a perfect homage to both the lavish celebrations and the understated, nourishing fare that mark the seasons in the Spring Court.

¼ cup honey, plus more for drizzling

1 sheet puff pastry, thawed if frozen

2 tablespoons roughly chopped fresh thyme leaves

Kosher salt

Freshly cracked black pepper, to taste

1 small yellow onion, thinly sliced into rounds

1 cup shaved Parmesan cheese

1 large egg, beaten

Preheat the oven to 400°F. Line a rimmed baking sheet with parchment paper.

Using the ¼-cup honey, drizzle small puddles of honey on the parchment-lined baking sheet, in three rows of four at intervals of about 4 inches.

Put the puff pastry on a work surface and cut it into 12 equal rectangles using a sharp paring knife.

Onto each honey puddle, sprinkle thyme leaves, dividing evenly, a pinch of kosher salt, and a bit of freshly cracked black pepper. Place a sliced onion round over each, followed by a generous amount of shaved Parmesan. Top with a rectangle of puff pastry.

Brush the top of each pastry with the beaten egg. Sprinkle lightly with additional salt.

Bake in the preheated oven until the tarts are nicely browned and puffed up, 15 to 18 minutes.

Remove the tarts from the oven and let them cool on the baking sheet for about 5 minutes. Then, using a spatula, carefully flip each tart over. Drizzle additional honey over each tart before serving. Serve warm.

MINTY SALAD WITH BROWN BUTTER AND SPICED HONEY VINAIGRETTE

This salad stands out from the crowd with its unique brown butter vinaigrette, a warm, nutty dressing that elevates the crisp, bitter greens. You might look at the quantity of fresh herbs and think, "A bit much?" but trust the process—this is a delicious salad that you'd find in the middle of Tamlin's dining table in the Spring Court. It's the perfect starter or side to many of the main courses in this book or makes a meal all on its own with a hearty bread such as Sopping Up Crusty Bread (page 85) on the side.

FOR THE DRESSING

¼ cup (½ stick) salted butter

½ teaspoon ground cumin

½ teaspoon fennel seeds

2 tablespoons honey, plus more to taste

1 tablespoon Dijon mustard

Juice of ½ lemon

FOR THE SALAD

2 cups mixed spring greens, chopped

1 cup radicchio, chopped

2 tablespoons chopped fresh mint

2 tablespoons chopped fresh parsley

2 tablespoons slivered almonds

To make the dressing, in a small saucepan, melt the butter over medium heat. Continue cooking, stirring frequently, until the butter begins to foam and brown bits appear at the bottom, 2 to 3 minutes. Stir in the cumin and fennel seeds. Cook until the spices are fragrant, about 30 seconds. Remove the saucepan from the heat. Add the 2 tablespoons honey, Dijon mustard, and lemon juice and whisk until blended. Taste the dressing and, if needed, add more honey to suit your preference.

Assemble the salad: In a large bowl, combine the chopped spring greens, radicchio, mint, parsley, and slivered almonds. Toss everything together.

Pour the prepared dressing over the salad. Using salad servers or clean hands, toss the salad again until all the ingredients are evenly coated with the dressing. Serve immediately. (If you plan to make the components ahead of time, keep the dressing and salad components separate until you're ready to eat. Reheat the dressing slightly before tossing it with the salad ingredients to ensure the butter is in liquid form, either by warming it over low heat on the stovetop or cooking in the microwave at 70% power for about 30 seconds.)

Autumn in Spring Crostini

Just like Lucien's own journey from the Autumn Court to the Spring Court, these bites balance the robust flavors of fall with the freshness of spring. They're a delicious representation of Lucien's multifaceted personality—a little bit of spice, a touch of sweetness, and an undeniable charm. Whether served as an appetizer or a bite at a cocktail party, these crostini are sure to spark conversations as vibrant as Lucien himself.

FOR THE CROSTINI

1 baguette

2 to 3 tablespoons olive oil

Kosher salt

FOR THE PUMPKIN SPREAD

4 ounces cream cheese, at room temperature

4 ounces soft goat cheese, at room temperature

½ cup pumpkin puree

¼ teaspoon kosher salt, plus more to taste

1 tablespoon pure maple syrup

¼ teaspoon cayenne pepper, plus more to taste

FOR THE GREENS

1 tablespoon olive oil

1 teaspoon pure maple syrup

1 tablespoon apple cider vinegar

¼ teaspoon kosher salt

2 cups arugula

Preheat the oven to 400°F. Line 2 baking sheets with parchment paper.

To make the crostini, slice the baguette on the bias into ¼-inch slices. Arrange the baguette sliced on the prepared baking sheets in a single layer. Lightly brush both sides of the slices with olive oil. Bake until golden brown on the first side, about 7 minutes, then flip the slices and bake until golden brown on the second side, another 3 to 5 minutes. Sprinkle lightly with salt. Let cool on the baking sheets.

To make the pumpkin spread, in the bowl of a stand mixer fitted with the whisk attachment, whip the cream cheese and goat cheese together on high speed until light and fluffy, about 2 minutes.

Add the pumpkin, salt, maple syrup, and cayenne pepper and continue to whip for 1 minute. Scrape down the sides with a spatula and continue to whip until ingredients are completely incorporated, about 2 minutes. Taste and adjust the salt and cayenne as desired.

To make the greens, in a large bowl, whisk together the olive oil, maple syrup, apple cider vinegar, and salt. Add the arugula and toss well.

To assemble, spread a generous amount of the pumpkin spread on each crostini, then top with the dressed arugula, dividing evenly. Serve immediately.

ADVICE FROM ALIS

Should you stumble upon crostini already prepared at the grocer's, do yourself a kindness and snatch them up to use in the stead of the homemade ones here, Dear.

Bites
from the Bone Carver's Lair

Welcome to the darker side of Prythian, where the villains and creatures that lurk in the shadows inspire recipes that are wickedly delicious. These snacks aren't for the faint of heart—they're culinary adventures that pay tribute to the fearsome beings that Feyre and company encounter. From the depths of the Court of Nightmares to the eerie lair of the Weaver, these recipes capture the essence of the tales that keep us on the edge of our seats.

Dare to try the Roasted Bone Marrow Spread with Garlic and Parmesan, a dish as rich and mysterious as the Bone Carver himself. Or take a bite out of the Wyrm's End Jalapeño Poppers, spicy enough to make even the most formidable fae sweat. For those who relish in the thrill of danger, The Weaver's Confit Drumsticks offer a taste of the sinister, while Attor's Wings on a Silver Platter delivers a dish best served cold, much like revenge.

So, gather your most daring friends, and let's toast to the creatures that make the night all the more interesting. After all, who says you can't enjoy the flavors inspired by the shadows? Just remember, keep an eye on your plate; in this part of the cookbook, you never know what might be lurking.

WYRM'S END
JALAPEÑO POPPERS

Enter the heat of battle with this appetizer, where each bite is as fiery as Feyre's showdown with the infamous Wyrm. Wrapped in bacon and secured with a toothpick that's as mighty as the bone Feyre used to slay the beast, these poppers are a tribute to epic victories. Forget ancient magic; these are all about the cream cheese and ranch mix, with cubes of cheddar that thankfully melt faster than Feyre's resolve in the face of danger. Grab a popper and let the crispy bacon and spicy jalapeño kickstart your own magical evening. If you can handle these, you're more than ready to take on a Wyrm—or at least the next chapter.

8 ounces cream cheese, softened

½ packet (1-ounce packet) ranch seasoning mix

4 ounces sharp Cheddar cheese, cut into ¼-inch cubes

12 jalapeño chiles, halved lengthwise, ribs and seeds removed

24 slices bacon

24 toothpicks, for assembly

Preheat the oven to 400°F. Line a rimmed baking sheet with aluminum foil and place a wire rack over the foil.

In a bowl, mix together the cream cheese and ranch seasoning mix until fully blended. Fold in the cubed cheddar cheese.

Spoon the cream cheese mixture into the jalapeño halves, dividing evenly. Wrap a slice of bacon around each filled jalapeño half, securing it with a toothpick.

Arrange the bacon-wrapped jalapeños on the wire rack on the prepared baking sheet. Bake in the preheated oven until the bacon is crispy and browned to your liking, 30 to 35 minutes.

Let cool for 5 minutes on the rack and serve.

ADVICE FROM ALIS

You might choose shredded cheese if it suits your fancy, but those wee cheese cubes turn your jalapeño poppers into an extra ooey-gooey delight, brimming with generous, melty pockets of cheese. Also, you might consider donning gloves whilst preparing the jalapeños, Dear, to protect your digits from their heat.

TRIO OF TRIALS DIP

This dip plays homage to the intense three-pronged challenge Feyre faced at Amarantha's hands. Starting with the earthy, Wyrm den–inspired white bean balsamic layer, it sets the stage for the stress of the second trial when Feyre realizes her illiteracy can have dire consequences, mirrored in the tangy, herb-infused goat cheese that brings a sense of Rhys's calming presence. The final layer is a fiery roasted red pepper and tomato blend, a vivid reminder of the blood-stained climax of the third trial. The perfect appetizer or snack for a watch party, make sure to serve this with Moon Phase Crackers (page 55).

FOR THE ROASTED TOMATO AND RED PEPPER DIP

20 ounces grape tomatoes

2 red bell peppers, quartered, cores and seeds removed

1 head garlic, top trimmed

6 tablespoons extra-virgin olive oil

½ teaspoon kosher salt, plus more to taste

2 teaspoons red wine vinegar

½ teaspoon smoked paprika

½ teaspoon crushed red pepper flakes, plus more to taste

For the roasted tomato and red pepper dip, preheat the oven to 325°F. On a rimmed baking sheet, arrange the tomatoes, bell peppers, and garlic. Drizzle with 4 tablespoons of the olive oil and sprinkle with the salt. Roast until the peppers are slightly blackened and the tomatoes are shriveled, 40 to 45 minutes. Transfer the roasted vegetables to a blender or clean food processor. Add the remaining 2 tablespoons olive oil, the red wine vinegar, smoked paprika, and red pepper flakes. Pulse until combined, yet slightly chunky. Season with additional salt and red pepper flakes to taste. Set aside until the assembly step, or if making in advance, cover the bowl with plastic wrap and refrigerate for up to 3 days.

FOR THE WHITE BEAN BALSAMIC DIP

One 15.5-ounce can cannellini beans, drained and rinsed

2 tablespoons extra-virgin olive oil

2 tablespoons balsamic vinegar

1 small garlic clove

½ teaspoon kosher salt

¼ teaspoon freshly ground black pepper

2–4 tablespoons water, if needed

FOR THE HERBY GOAT CHEESE DIP

6 ounces soft goat cheese, at room temperature

4 ounces cream cheese, at room temperature

1 to 2 tablespoons extra-virgin olive oil

1 tablespoon chopped fresh rosemary

¼ teaspoon kosher salt, plus more to taste

¼ teaspoon freshly cracked black pepper, plus more to tasted

Moon Phase Crackers (page 55), for serving

For the white bean dip, in a food processor, combine the cannellini beans, olive oil, balsamic vinegar, garlic, salt, and pepper. Process until smooth, adding water as needed to achieve desired consistency. Set aside until the assembly step, or if making in advance, cover the bowl with plastic wrap and refrigerate for up to 3 days.

For the herby goat cheese dip, in a clean food processor, combine the goat cheese, cream cheese, 1 tablespoon olive oil, rosemary, salt, and pepper. Process until creamy and fluffy. If needed, add the remaining tablespoon of olive oil to thin and process until combined. Taste and adjust the salt and pepper as desired. Set aside until the assembly step, or if making in advance, cover the bowl with plastic wrap and refrigerate for up to 3 days.

To assemble, in a clear glass 8- or 10-inch dish with high sides, layer the dips starting with the White Bean Balsamic Dip, followed by the Herby Goat Cheese Dip, and topped with the Roasted Tomato and Red Pepper Dip. Serve cold or at room temperature, accompanied by the Moon Phase Crackers.

Roasted Bone Marrow Spread with Garlic and Parmesan

YIELDS

8

SERVINGS

Roasting marrow bones might sound like a task for an ancient, all-knowing being like the Bone Carver himself, but don't worry they're shockingly easy to prepare. Mixed with Parmesan and parsley, this rich, buttery spread is a nod to the enigmatic character's ability to carve destiny from bones. Serve it up with Sopping Up Crusty Bread (page 85) for an appetizer that's as intriguing as the legends of the Old Gods themselves. It's delicious on either soft or toasted bread!

5 beef marrow bones, each 3 to 5 inches long

1 head garlic

1 tablespoon olive oil

Kosher salt, to taste

2 tablespoons freshly grated Parmigiano-Reggiano cheese

1 tablespoon chopped fresh flat leaf parsley

Sopping Up Crusty Bread (page 85)

ADVICE FROM ALIS

While you might not find them at your usual market, marrow bones are often readily at hand if you visit your local butcher, Dear.

Preheat the oven to 400°F.

Cut the top off the garlic head and place it on a piece of foil. Drizzle with olive oil and sprinkle with salt. Wrap the garlic in the foil and roast until cloves are soft and fragrant, 30 to 45 minutes. Remove from the oven and set aside to cool.

Increase the oven temperature to 450°F. Line a rimmed baking sheet with foil.

Place the marrow bones on the baking sheet vertically if whole, marrow-side up if cut in half. Bake in the preheated oven until the marrow is soft and spreadable but not liquid, 15 to 25 minutes. The cooking time may vary; you may need to remove smaller marrow bones at 15 minutes and let larger ones cook for the full 25 minutes.

Use a knife or small spoon to scoop the marrow from the bones into a bowl. Discard the bones or save to make a stock (they will freeze well). Squeeze the garlic cloves from the roasted head into the same bowl. Stir in the Parmesan cheese and parsley. Season with additional salt to taste. (If the marrow hardens during this process, cook it in the microwave at 50% power for 15 to 30 seconds.)

Serve spread on Sopping Up Crusty Bread as an appetizer or side dish.

PULL–APART
BREAD WREATH WITH PESTO AND SUNDRIED TOMATOES

Imagine yourself in the Court of Nightmares with this bread wreath, where the lavish spreads of this dark court come to life in your own kitchen. Imagine a bread so rich with pesto and sun-dried tomatoes that it distracts and dazzles, much like Feyre and Rhys's own performance on the High Lord's throne in *A Court of Mist and Fury*. Simple to bake and perfect for sharing, this dish is a nod to the bold and the brave.

FOR THE FILLING

½ cup (1 stick) salted butter, at room temperature

½ cup prepared basil pesto

½ cup oil-packed sun-dried tomatoes

⅓ cup freshly grated Parmigiano-Reggiano cheese

FOR THE BREAD WREATH

Two 13.8-ounce cans refrigerated pizza dough

All-purpose flour, for rolling

Flaky sea salt

Dried Italian seasoning

Lightly grease a Bundt pan with butter.

To make the filling, in a bowl, mix together the butter, pesto, sun-dried tomatoes, and Parmesan cheese. Set aside.

On a lightly floured work surface, use a rolling pin to roll out the pizza dough into 2 large rectangles, each about ¼-inch thick.

Spread the filling mixture evenly over the dough rectangles, dividing evenly. Using a pizza cutter or sharp knife, cut each dough rectangle into 12 squares (or as close to squares as possible) and stack them, 6 per stack. Place the stacked dough rectangles edges up in the prepared Bundt pan. Repeat with the remaining dough pieces to make a ring. Cover the pan with a clean dish towel and let it rise in a warm place for at least 1 hour and up to 3 hours; the longer it rises the better when using store-bought pizza dough.

Preheat the oven to 350°F.

Bake the bread in the preheated oven until golden brown, 30 to 40 minutes. Let cool in the pan for 10 to 15 minutes before turning out onto a large round platter. Sprinkle with sea salt and dried Italian seasoning before serving.

WALL WATCH
CHICKEN CAPRESE SANDWICHES

Picture Feyre and Lucien, trekking through the forests with the King of Hybern's minions in tow, munching on these sandwiches as if they haven't got a care in the world—aside from the occasional evil twin or the task of plotting the downfall of their enemies, of course. It's the perfect snack for planning your next big move or just pretending you're on a high-stakes mission in your own backyard. Tucked between slices of crusty French bread, each sandwich features layers of pesto mayo, creamy mozzarella, and juicy tomatoes—a bold trio that's as ready for adventure as Feyre herself.

FOR THE CHICKEN

¼ cup balsamic vinegar

1 tablespoon olive oil

1 tablespoon dried Italian seasoning

4 cloves garlic, minced

½ teaspoon kosher salt

½ teaspoon crushed red pepper flakes (optional)

¼ teaspoon freshly cracked black pepper

1 pound boneless, skinless chicken breasts

FOR THE SALAD

1 tablespoon olive oil

2 tablespoons balsamic vinegar

¼ teaspoon kosher salt

¼ teaspoon freshly cracked black pepper

4 cups arugula

In a bowl, whisk together the vinegar, oil, Italian seasoning, garlic, salt, pepper flakes (if using), and black pepper to create the marinade. Put the chicken in a large resealable plastic bag or airtight container and pour the marinade over it. Make sure the chicken is fully coated. Refrigerate for at least 1 hour or up to overnight.

Prepare an outdoor charcoal grill with medium-hot coals or preheat a gas grill to medium high. Or warm a stovetop grill pan over medium-high heat. Grill the chicken breasts on each side, until the chicken is cooked through and no longer pink inside, 7 to 8 minutes. (Alternatively, to roast the chicken, preheat the oven to 450°F. Line a rimmed baking sheet with aluminum foil. Place the chicken on the prepared baking sheet and roast until the chicken is cooked through and no longer pink inside, 15 to 18 minutes.) Let the chicken rest for 5 minutes before slicing into ½-inch-thick slices.

To make the salad, in a large bowl, whisk together olive oil, balsamic vinegar, salt, and pepper. Add the arugula and toss to coat. Set aside.

In a small bowl, mix together the pesto and mayonnaise. Set aside.

Continued

FOR THE SANDWICHES

⅓ cup prepared
basil pesto

¼ cup mayonnaise

1 baguette

8 ounces fresh mozzarella
cheese, thinly sliced

½ pound ripe tomatoes
(beefsteak, heirloom, or
roma), thinly sliced

Slice the baguette in half lengthwise. Spread the pesto-mayo mixture over both cut sides of the bread. Layer the salad on the bottom half of the baguette, then add the sliced grilled chicken, mozzarella cheese, and tomato slices on top. Add the top half of the baguette. Cut into sandwich-sized pieces. These can vary in size depending on how you're serving them: smaller for a cocktail or tea party, larger for lunches. Serve at room temperature.

ADVICE FROM ALIS
You could prepare the chicken early, Love, and then put together the sandwiches when the time is right.

ATTOR'S WINGS
ON A SILVER PLATTER

These wings are a culinary tribute to Feyre's brave encounter with the Attor—the very moment that crowned her as the "Defender of the Rainbow." Inspired by the Attor's shadowy essence, they bring a mix of heat and smoky flavor to your table. So, serve these wings up on a silver platter and relive Feyre's triumph over one of Prythian's most feared creatures.

FOR THE WINGS

¼ cup cornstarch

2 teaspoons kosher salt

½ teaspoon freshly cracked black pepper

2 pounds party-style chicken wings (flats and drumettes separated)

FOR THE SAUCE

¼ cup (½ stick) salted butter

4 cloves garlic, minced

2 teaspoons chili powder

1 teaspoon smoked paprika

½ teaspoon cayenne pepper

¼ teaspoon ground cinnamon

Preheat the oven to 450°F. Line 2 rimmed baking sheets with foil and place a wire rack on top of each.

To make the wings, in a large bowl, mix together the cornstarch, salt, and black pepper. Add the chicken wings and toss to coat evenly. Arrange the wings on the wire racks on the prepared baking sheets. Bake in the preheated oven for 10 minutes, then flip the wings. Continue baking until they are golden brown and crispy, 8 to 10 minutes.

While the wings are baking, prepare the sauce. In a small saucepan over medium heat, melt the butter. Add the minced garlic and cook for 1 minute. Reduce the heat to low and add the chili powder, smoked paprika, cayenne pepper, and cinnamon. Cook until the mixture becomes fragrant, stirring constantly, 1 to 2 minutes.

Using tongs, transfer the wings to a large bowl. Pour the prepared sauce over the wings and toss to coat them thoroughly. Serve the wings hot.

THE WEAVER'S
CONFIT DRUMSTICKS

Get ready to cook up a dish that would make even the Weaver of the Wood pause in her sinister pursuits. These olive oil–poached chicken drumsticks, infused with garlic, rosemary, and thyme, are so tender and flavorful, they could almost be a product of chthonic magic themselves. While they're inspired by the Weaver's rather creepy abode, fear not—there's no dark magic required, and you can rest assured that no intruders were harmed in the making of this recipe.

10 chicken drumsticks

Kosher salt

Freshly cracked black pepper

5 sprigs fresh thyme, plus more for serving (optional)

3 sprigs fresh rosemary, plus more for serving (optional)

1 head garlic, top cut off

4 cups olive oil

Preheat the oven to 250ºF.

Season the chicken drumsticks generously with salt and pepper. For best results, cover, and refrigerate for 1 to 2 hours before cooking.

Arrange the seasoned drumsticks in a 9-by-13-inch baking dish. Tuck the sprigs of thyme and rosemary around the chicken. Place the head of garlic, cut side up, on top of the chicken or alongside it. Carefully pour the olive oil over the chicken, ensuring some oil covers the head of garlic. Bake in the preheated oven for 45 minutes. Turn the drumsticks, then bake until the drumsticks are completely golden, about 45 more minutes.

Remove the baking dish from the oven. Carefully extract the head of garlic and when cool enough to handle, squeeze the softened garlic cloves into a large bowl. Using a fork, mash the garlic. Spoon a couple of tablespoons of the cooking oil from the baking dish into the bowl and mix with the garlic to form a paste. Add the warm chicken drumsticks to the bowl and toss them in the garlic paste with tongs, ensuring they are well coated.

If using, arrange fresh sprigs of rosemary and thyme on a large serving platter. Place the garlic-coated drumsticks on top of the herbs. Serve the drumsticks warm.

Moon Phase
CRACKERS

Get ready to unleash your inner High Priestess with these moon-shaped crackers inspired by the cunning Ianthe. With their golden hue and celestial shapes, these crackers are a nod to her moon cycle tattoo. They're ideal for eating while scheming your next move in the game of courts. So, whether you're attempting to seduce a High Lord or just craving a deliciously crisp bite, these crackers make the perfect snack. Enjoy them on their own or serve with the Trio of Trials Dip (page 42).

2 cups all-purpose flour

½ teaspoon kosher salt, plus more for topping

¼ teaspoon freshly cracked black pepper

1 cup grated Parmesan cheese, plus more for topping

⅓ cup cold salted butter, cut into ½-inch cubes

½ cup milk (whole, 2%, or 1%)

Dried Italian seasoning for topping

Preheat the oven to 400°F. Line 3 baking sheets with parchment paper. (If you don't have 3 baking sheets, you can work in batches.)

In a mixing bowl, combine the flour, salt, pepper, and Parmesan. Add the cold butter cubes. Using a fork or a pastry cutter, work the butter into the flour mixture until the mixture becomes crumbly, with no large butter chunks remaining. While either stirring with a spatula or using a mixer fitted with a paddle attachment on low speed, gradually drizzle in the milk just until the dough starts to come together.

Form the dough into a ball and knead it briefly to bring it together. Divide the dough into 3 equal portions. Take 1 portion of dough and flatten it into a square on a lightly floured work surface. Using a rolling pin, roll it out to about a 10-inch square that is about ⅛ inch thick. Using a small round pastry cutter, cut out shapes for full moons, half-moons, and crescent moons. Gather any dough scraps, re-roll, and continue cutting out shapes. As you work, place the shapes on the prepared baking sheets, spacing them close together. Repeat the rolling and cutting process with the remaining dough portions.

Sprinkle each dough shape with a pinch of kosher salt, Parmesan cheese, and dried Italian seasoning, then bake until the crackers are just golden brown, 12 to 15 minutes.

Remove the crackers from the oven and allow them to cool on the baking sheets for 10 to 15 minutes. Once cooled, store the crackers in an airtight container at room temperature.

Feasts
Fit for High Fae

Step into the grand dining halls of Prythian and prepare to feast like the High Fae. The recipes in this section bring the flavors of a world where magic meets the mundane and every meal tells a tale. Whether it's a dish sparked by starlight, or a simple, comforting soup shared in a moment of vulnerability, these recipes are your tickets to the lavish dinners and cozy suppers of our beloved characters.

Imagine butter-poached salmon that whisks you away to a critical gathering in the human lands, or let slow-roasted chicken evoke the rustic, homey feel of a meal shared among friends. Each dish, from the Starlit Stuffed Chicken with Berry Reduction in honor of Nyx's birth to The House's Hearty Pork and Bean Stew, is a nod to the memorable moments that define the series. With every bite, you'll traverse the realms of Prythian, from the vibrant streets of Velaris to the mysterious depths of the Court of Nightmares.

These recipes are an invitation to wield your spatula and conjure dishes that could easily grace the tables of a High Lord's (or Lady's) manor. So, gather your court, set the table, and let's raise a glass to the feasts that fuel the adventures, the heartaches, and the triumphs of our favorite High Fae. After all, in Prythian, a meal is never just a meal—it's a saga waiting to be savored.

"WELCOME TO SPRING"
SAUCY LEMON CHICKEN

Ready for a recipe that echoes the very first meal Feyre had in Prythian? Imagine sitting at that grand table, unsure if the food might be laced with something otherworldly, yet unable to resist the tempting smell of meats and sauces as you try to get a feel for your captors and their home. This recipe aims to capture that moment—chicken breasts bathed in a zesty garlic-laced lemon sauce and topped with a tangy caper relish. It's best enjoyed with a side of Sopping Up Crusty Bread (page 85) and a glass of sparkling Faerie Wine (page 139).

FOR THE CAPER RELISH

2 tablespoons brined capers, drained and roughly chopped

¼ cup chopped fresh flat leaf parsley

Finely grated zest of 1 lemon

FOR THE CHICKEN

4 large boneless, skinless chicken breasts

Kosher salt

Freshly cracked black pepper

½ teaspoon garlic powder

½ cup all-purpose flour

4 tablespoons (½ stick) salted butter

1 tablespoon olive oil

¼ cup dry white wine

2 tablespoons fresh lemon juice (from about 1 lemon)

½ cup heavy cream

¼ cup chicken broth

To make the caper relish, in a small bowl, mix together the capers, parsley, and lemon zest. Set aside until ready to serve.

To make the chicken, cut the chicken breasts in half horizontally (as if you are butterflying them) all the way through to make 8 wide, thin pieces. Trim away any excess fat. Season the chicken generously with salt and pepper.

In a shallow bowl, mix together the flour and garlic powder. Dredge each chicken piece in the flour mixture, coating both sides.

In a large skillet over medium-high heat, melt 2 tablespoons of the butter with the olive oil. When hot, add the chicken in batches and cook until golden, 4 to 5 minutes per side. Transfer to a plate. Repeat with remaining chicken pieces.

Remove the skillet from the heat. Add the wine and lemon juice, scraping up any brown bits from the pan with a wooden spoon. Stir in the remaining 2 tablespoons butter, the heavy cream, and the chicken broth and place over medium-low heat. Once the liquid is simmering, return all the chicken to the pan.

Cook until the chicken is cooked through, and the sauce has reduced, until it coats the back of a wooden spoon, 7 to 10 minutes. If the sauce thickens too much, add a bit more chicken broth.

Transfer the chicken to a platter and serve warm, topped with the caper relish.

Merchant's
Spiced Chicken Pie

YIELDS
6-8
SERVINGS

Let's go on a journey inspired by the travels of the legendary merchant, Mr. Archeron himself, whose trading career saw both highs and lows. Although we don't know exactly what he traded, he may have traded in spices, and that inspired this dish. This chicken pie has a blend of aromatic spices, succulent chicken, and sweet potatoes encased in a golden crust. With every savory bite, celebrate the merchant's enduring spirit and how he ultimately came through for his daughters. This recipe is a playful homage to a life well-seasoned.

2 prepared, unbaked refrigerated piecrust sheets

1 tablespoon coconut oil

1 yellow onion, finely diced

4 cloves garlic, minced

½-inch knob fresh ginger, peeled and minced

1½ teaspoons ground turmeric

1 teaspoon ground cumin

1 teaspoon ground cinnamon

1 teaspoon ground coriander

½ teaspoon cayenne pepper

1 sweet potato (about ½ pound), peeled and diced into 1-inch cubes

1½ cups full fat coconut milk

3 roma tomatoes, diced

1 pound boneless, skinless chicken breasts

2 tablespoons salted butter, melted

Kosher salt, to taste

Preheat the oven to 425ºF.

Press one of the piecrusts into a standard 9-inch pie dish. Set aside.

In a large Dutch oven or stockpot, melt the coconut oil over medium heat. Add the onion, garlic, and ginger and cook, stirring occasionally, until they soften and become fragrant, 2 to 3 minutes.

Add the turmeric, cumin, cinnamon, coriander, and cayenne. Continue to cook, stirring occasionally, for an additional minute. Stir in the sweet potato, coconut milk, diced tomatoes, and chicken breasts. Increase the heat to medium-high and bring the mixture to a simmer. Reduce to medium-low. Allow it to simmer until the chicken is cooked through, about 15 minutes. Remove the pot from the heat.

Remove the chicken from the pot and place it on a work surface. Using 2 forks, pull the chicken apart to shred. Return the shredded chicken to the pot and stir to mix it with the other ingredients.

Ladle the chicken and sauce into the piecrust-lined dish. Cover it with the second piecrust, lining up the edges, and trimming any excess dough. Seal the edges by crimping them together with your fingertips. To allow steam to escape during baking, make several small slits in the top crust.

Brush the top crust with the melted butter and lightly sprinkle it with kosher salt.

Bake the pie in the preheated oven until the crust is golden brown, 30 to 35 minutes. Allow the pie to rest for 10 minutes before slicing and serving.

Butter-Poached Salmon with Dill and Lemon

Step into the world of Feyre's family's estate in the mortal lands, where tensions ran high during a crucial dinner meeting. This recipe captures the essence of that memorable evening, featuring a delightful combination of zesty lemon and fresh dill that perfectly complements buttery salmon. Pair it with Cheesy Chive Mashed Potatoes (page 95) for a complete meal, just like the one that played a pivotal role in preparing for the war with Hybern.

One 8- to 10-ounce salmon fillet

Kosher salt

¼ cup (½ stick) salted butter

1 tablespoon fresh lemon juice (from about ½ lemon)

1 tablespoon chopped fresh dill

Season the salmon fillet lightly with salt.

In a heavy-duty skillet over medium heat, melt the butter. Place the salmon fillet in the skillet, skin side down, and cook until the skin is just golden, about 2 minutes. Carefully flip the salmon using a spatula and cook until the salmon is just flaky when tested with the tip of a knife, an additional 2 minutes, or until cooked to your liking. Turn off the heat and transfer the seared salmon to a serving plate.

Stir the lemon juice and fresh dill into the melted butter in the skillet to make a sauce. Spoon the lemon-dill butter sauce over the salmon. Serve immediately.

Townhouse
Slow-Roasted Chicken
with Sage and Lemon

At the relaxed dinners at the Townhouse, a roasted chicken often finds its place at the center of the table. This recipe is a straightforward yet delicious main dish, featuring flavors of sage and lemon. The golden, crispy skin and tender meat make this chicken a classic choice for an evening of shared stories and laughter, not to mention plenty of Faerie Wine. Served with a garlicky pan sauce, you'll be grateful you don't have to battle Cassian for seconds.

One 3½- to 4-pound whole chicken

Kosher salt

Freshly cracked black pepper

¼ cup salted butter, at room temperature

2 tablespoons chopped fresh sage

2 lemons, cut into slices

1 head garlic, top cut off (skin left on)

Olive oil

6 bunches of fresh sage, for garnish

Juice of 1 lemon

ADVICE FROM ALIS
Should you find yourself at odds with spatchcocking the chicken, there are a wealth of instructional videos online to guide you, Love.

Preheat your oven to 325°F.

Remove the neck, loose skin, and any giblets from the chicken and discard them. Remove the backbone from the chicken with sharp kitchen shears, then flip over the bird, and crack the breastbone so it can lie flat (this is called "spatchcocking" a chicken). Insert your fingers under the skin of the breasts and thighs to loosen the membranes. Pat the chicken dry with paper towels. Season the bird generously with salt and pepper.

In a small bowl, mix together the butter and sage. Rub the butter mixture all over the chicken, ensuring to get both on and under the skin. Tuck a few lemon slices under the skin. Arrange the remaining lemon slices on an ungreased rimmed baking sheet. Place the chicken on top of the lemon slices. Nestle the head of garlic on the baking sheet next to the bird. Drizzle both the chicken and garlic with olive oil.

Roast the chicken in the preheated oven until an instant-read thermometer inserted into the thickest part of a thigh registers 165°F, about 2 ½ hours. While the chicken is roasting, arrange the sage bunches on a serving platter and set aside.

Transfer the roasted chicken to the platter on top of the sage leaves. Cover with foil and let it rest for 10 minutes, up to 30 minutes.

While the chicken rests, squeeze the roasted garlic cloves from their skins into a small saucepan. Add the pan drippings from the baking sheet and the juice of 1 lemon. Whisk over low heat until the garlic cloves have dissolved.

Carve the chicken into breast, thigh, drumstick, and wing pieces on the platter. Serve accompanied by the pan sauce.

CREAMY
CHICKEN AND
WILD RICE SOUP

YIELDS

6

SERVINGS

When life dishes out a beating, whip up this hearty soup to mend body and soul. Inspired by Cassian's brawl with Rhysand to let the High Lord blow off some steam in *A Court of Silver Flames,* this soup's like a comforting hug after a rough day. Tender chicken meets wild rice along with savory vegetables and a light lemon cream broth in a bowl that'll soothe your spirit—just like it did for our favorite Night Court troublemakers. Grab a spoon, tear off a chunk of Sopping Up Crusty Bread (page 85), and heal, one tasty spoonful at a time.

4 tablespoons (½ stick) salted butter

1 yellow onion, diced

3 carrots, peeled and diced

3 stalks celery, diced

3 cloves garlic, minced

1 teaspoon kosher salt

¼ cup all-purpose flour

6 cups chicken broth

1 tablespoon poultry seasoning

½ teaspoon freshly cracked black pepper

1 cup wild rice blend

1 pound boneless, skinless chicken breasts

1 cup heavy cream

Juice of ½ lemon

Sopping Up Crusty Bread (page 85)

In a Dutch oven or stockpot, melt 1 tablespoon of the butter over medium heat. Add the onion, carrots, celery, and garlic. Cook, stirring occasionally, until the vegetables begin to soften, 2 to 3 minutes. Season with salt and stir. Add the remaining 3 tablespoons butter and the flour. Cook, stirring frequently, for 1 minute. Add the chicken broth, poultry seasoning, and pepper. Increase the heat to medium-high and bring the mixture to a simmer, stirring frequently. Reduce the heat to medium-low and add the chicken breasts and wild rice.

Cover the pot with a lid, leaving it slightly ajar to allow steam to escape, and simmer, stirring occasionally, until the chicken and wild rice are fully cooked, 35 to 40 minutes. Remove from heat.

Remove the chicken breasts from the pot and place them on a cutting board. Using 2 forks, pull the chicken breasts apart to form shreds. Return the shredded chicken to the pot.

Stir in the heavy cream and lemon juice. Taste and adjust the seasoning with salt and pepper, if necessary.

To serve, ladle the soup among serving bowls and serve hot accompanied by bread.

Rosemary and Garlic Roast Beef with Creamy Horseradish Sauce

YIELDS
8
SERVINGS

Get ready to bring a touch of Prythian-style feasting to your dinner table with this juicy roast beef recipe. Perfectly seasoned and butter-basted, it's a hearty centerpiece that'll have your guests feeling like they're dining in a grand hall, minus any High Fae. And if by some miracle there's any left, it makes for an excellent cold roast beef sandwich the next day. Just don't forget to hide some away before your guests devour it all!

FOR THE ROAST

¼ cup (½ stick) salted butter, at room temperature

5 cloves garlic, minced

1 tablespoon chopped fresh rosemary

1 tablespoon kosher salt

1 teaspoon freshly cracked black pepper

One 4 pound beef Eye of Round Roast

FOR THE CREAMY HORSERADISH SAUCE

½ cup sour cream

¼ cup mayonnaise

2 tablespoons prepared horseradish, drained

1 tablespoon Dijon mustard

1 tablespoon finely chopped chives

1 teaspoon white vinegar

½ teaspoon kosher salt

¼ teaspoon freshly cracked black pepper

Preheat the oven to 450°F. Fit a roasting pan with a roasting rack. (Alternatively, line a rimmed baking sheet with foil and place a wire rack on top.)

In a small bowl, combine the butter, garlic, rosemary, salt, and pepper and mix well.

Pat the beef dry with paper towels. Rub the butter mixture evenly over the entire surface of the beef. Place the beef on the prepared roasting rack. Roast in the preheated oven for 15 minutes, then reduce the heat to 325°F. Continue roasting until an instant-read thermometer inserted into the center of the beef reads 130°F, about 1 hour and 15 minutes more for medium doneness, or until done to your liking.

Remove the beef from the oven, tent with a foil, and allow it to rest for 15 to 30 minutes before slicing.

While the beef cooks, make the Creamy Horseradish Sauce. Mix together all ingredients in a medium-size bowl. For best results, cover and let sit for 30 minutes before serving. If making in advance, cover and refrigerate until ready to serve.

Cut the beef into ½-inch slices and arrange on a platter. Spoon pan juices from the roasting pan over the sliced beef and serve. Offer Creamy Horseradish Sauce alongside.

Artist's Palette
Vegetable Gratin

Step into the kaleidoscopic charm of Velaris's Rainbow Quarter with this colorful dish, inspired by Feyre's passion for painting. Each layer of vibrant sweet potatoes, summer squash, zucchini, red cabbage, and parsnips is a nod to the hues on her painter's palette. Covered in a creamy Gouda cheese sauce that melts into every layer, it's not just a feast for the eyes but a tribute to Feyre's artistry. Perfect as a vegetarian main course or a decadent side dish, this casserole brings a piece of Feyre's world right to your table.

2 tablespoons butter, for greasing the baking dish

1 garnet sweet potato, peeled

1 large yellow summer squash, ends trimmed

1 large zucchini or 2 small zucchini, ends trimmed

2 parsnips, peeled and ends trimmed

½ red cabbage, outer leaves removed

Kosher salt

FOR THE BECHAMEL SAUCE

¼ cup salted butter

4 cloves garlic, minced

¼ cup all-purpose flour

1 cup vegetable broth

1 cup milk (any milk)

1 cup heavy cream

1 teaspoon kosher salt

½ teaspoon freshly cracked black pepper

1 teaspoon dried oregano

2 cups grated gouda cheese

¼ cup grated Parmigiano-Reggiano cheese

Preheat the oven to 350°F. Grease a 9-by-13-inch baking dish with butter.

Using a mandolin or a food processor fitted with the 2mm slicer attachment, slice the sweet potato, summer squash, zucchini, and parsnips into thin rounds. (Alternatively, use a very sharp knife.) Place the halved cabbage flat side down on the cutting board and slice it into ½-inch strips. Place each vegetable in separate paper towel–lined bowls. Toss each vegetable with a sprinkle of kosher salt and set aside.

To make the bechamel sauce, melt the butter in a large skillet over medium heat. Add the garlic and cook until fragrant, about 1 minute. Whisk in the flour and cook, stirring constantly, until it begins to turn golden, 2 to 3 minutes. Reduce the heat to medium-low and gradually add the vegetable broth, milk, and heavy cream. Continue whisking until the mixture thickens, about 5 minutes. Remove from the heat and stir in the salt, pepper, oregano, and gouda cheese until the cheese is fully melted.

Squeeze any excess liquid from the vegetables using the paper towels. In the prepared baking dish, layer parsnips, followed by the cabbage and then zucchini. Pour over half of the bechamel sauce, spreading it to the edges. Top with a layer each of the summer squash and sweet potatoes. Cover with the remaining bechamel sauce, spreading it out to the edges.

Bake in the preheated oven for 30 minutes. Remove the dish from the oven and sprinkle grated Parmesan over the top. Return to the oven and bake until the vegetables are tender and the Parmesan is golden, 15 to 20 minutes.

Let cool for 5 to 10 minutes, then cut into squares and serve with a spatula.

SEVENDA'S SPICED
VEGETARIAN STEW

Sevenda always serves meals that are rich, savory, and well-spiced in her Velaris restaurant. This stew, with its blend of spices and creamy coconut milk, is meant to make you feel like you're dining along the Sidra under the stars. Each spoonful is a burst of flavor and warmth, a comforting embrace in a bowl, just as Sevenda intended. Serve it with the Sunny Rice Pilaf (page 92) for a complete meal.

FOR THE VEGETARIAN STEW

2 tablespoons ghee

1 yellow onion, diced

2-inch piece fresh ginger, peeled and minced

3 garlic cloves, minced

1 teaspoon ground coriander

1 teaspoon ground cumin

1 teaspoon ground turmeric

½ teaspoon crushed red pepper flakes

1½ pounds sweet potatoes, peeled and diced into 1-inch pieces

½ cup red lentils, picked over

½ teaspoon kosher salt, plus more to taste

¼ teaspoon freshly cracked black pepper, plus more to taste

4 cups vegetable broth

One 13.5-ounce can full-fat coconut milk

1 small bunch kale, cleaned, stemmed, and torn into 1-inch pieces

To make the vegetarian stew, in a large stockpot or Dutch oven over medium heat, melt 1 tablespoon of the ghee. Add the onion and sauté, stirring occasionally, until translucent and soft, about 5 minutes. Add the ginger and garlic and cook for an additional minute. Stir in the remaining 1 tablespoon ghee, the coriander, cumin, turmeric, and crushed red pepper flakes. Cook, stirring frequently, until the spices are fragrant, about 1 minute.

Add the sweet potatoes and lentils to the pot, stirring to coat them with the spices. Stir in the salt, black pepper, and vegetable broth, scraping up any browned bits from the bottom of the pot. Increase the heat to medium-high and bring the mixture to a boil. Then reduce the heat to medium-low and simmer with the lid slightly ajar, until the sweet potatoes are soft when pierced with a fork, about 20 minutes.

Stir the coconut milk and kale into the stew. Simmer until the kale is wilted and bright green, about 5 minutes. Taste and adjust the salt and pepper as needed.

Continued

**FOR THE
SPICY GHEE TOPPING**

3 tablespoons ghee

*½ teaspoon crushed
red pepper flakes*

*Chopped fresh cilantro,
for garnish*

*Plain full-fat yogurt,
for garnish*

To make the spicy ghee, melt the ghee in a small saucepan over medium-low heat. Add the crushed red pepper flakes and cook, stirring frequently, until the pepper flakes are fragrant, 30 to 60 seconds, being careful not to burn the flakes. Set aside.

To serve, ladle the stew into serving bowls and serve hot, garnished with chopped cilantro, a dollop of plain yogurt, and a drizzle of spicy ghee.

ADVICE FROM ALIS

Ghee, that's clarified butter, is found in jars usually nestled near the international aisle at your grocery store. Should it prove elusive, butter will serve just as well, Dear.

CIDER–BRAISED
PORK SHOULDER,
HEWN CITY STYLE

You've stepped into the Court of Nightmares, where banquet tables are laden with an extravagant array of foods. Among the spread are roast meats, fruits, and ciders. This recipe invites you to recreate a piece of the feast: tender pork shoulder slowly braised in apple cider and fresh herbs. It promises to be a star at your own gathering, minus the palpable tension of the Hewn City.

One 4- to 5-pound pork shoulder or Boston butt

Kosher salt

Freshly cracked black pepper

2 tablespoons olive oil

2 cups apple cider

2 cups chicken broth

2 tablespoons Dijon mustard

1 shallot, diced

1 head garlic, top sliced off to expose cloves

3 sprigs fresh rosemary

4 sprigs fresh thyme

1 red onion, cut into thick slices lengthwise

2 Granny Smith apples, peeled and cut into thick slices

Preheat the oven to 325°F.

Trim any excess fat from the pork, cutting away large fat caps. Cut the pork into 2 to 3 large chunks. Season generously with salt and pepper.

In a large Dutch oven, heat the olive oil over medium-high heat. Once hot, add the pork in a single layer and sear until browned on all sides, 4 to 5 minutes per side, working in batches if necessary. Don't overcrowd the Dutch oven or the pork will not brown.

While the pork sears, whisk together the apple cider, chicken broth, and mustard. Set aside. Use kitchen twine to tie the rosemary and thyme into a bundle.

Pour the apple cider mixture into the Dutch oven. (If you browned the pork in batches, add the rest of the pork back to the pan). Stir with a wooden spoon and scrape up the browned bits on the bottom of the pan. Add the herb bundle and whole garlic head. Cover and transfer it to the preheated oven.

Braise the pork in the covered pan in the oven until it is fork-tender, 3 to 4 hours, flipping the pork pieces halfway through the cooking time. Start checking for tenderness at 2 hours.

Continued

Once the pork is fork-tender, carefully remove the pot from the oven, uncover it, then add the red onion slices and apple wedges to the pot. Cover and return to the oven until the apples have just softened, another 15 minutes.

Remove the pot from the oven and let the pork rest in the liquid for 30 minutes.

Serve the pork with the cooking juices spooned over, accompanied by the apples and onions. Squeeze the garlic cloves out of their skins into the broth or onto the pork if desired.

ADVICE FROM ALIS

If it suits your fancy, a cast iron or stout skillet may stand in for the Dutch oven to sear the pork.

To bring this recipe to life in a slow cooker, carry on with the instructions until you've seared the pork. Once it's nicely browned, shift the pork over to your slow cooker. Pour atop the apple cider blend, then tuck in the bundle of herbs and the head of garlic. Let it simmer on low for a stretch of 6 to 8 hours. From there, resume with the directions beginning, "Once the pork is fork-tender," Dear.

Beef Stew,
If the Cook's to Be Believed

As Rhysand returns to their room at the Inn with a tray, Feyre is surprised to smell something delicious. "Rabbit stew, if the cook's to be believed," he quips. This recipe is inspired by that moment in the book, though we've opted for beef here—it's much easier to find and just as hearty. There they are, nestled in a room that's a tight fit for just the bed, let alone a dining space, sharing a stew that promises to warm more than just their stomachs in the quaint setup. So, get a spoon and get ready: the stew isn't the only thing bringing the heat in that cozy room. Choose a delicious bread to go with the stew, such as the Cheese and Chive Scones (page 22) or Sopping Up Crusty Bread (page 85).

2 to 3 pounds beef chuck roast, cut into 1-inch cubes

Kosher salt

Freshly cracked black pepper

½ cup all-purpose flour

2 tablespoons olive oil, plus more if needed

1 yellow onion, thinly sliced

5 cloves garlic, minced

3 carrots, peeled and diced

⅓ cup dry red wine

One 6-ounce can tomato paste

4 cups beef broth

4 large red potatoes (about 2 pounds), diced

1 tablespoon chopped fresh thyme

½ teaspoon dried oregano

1 tablespoon Worcestershire sauce

Cheese and Chive Scones (page 22) or Sopping Up Crusty Bread (page 85) for accompaniment

Season the beef cubes generously with salt and pepper. Transfer them to a large bowl and sprinkle with the flour, tossing to coat them evenly.

In a large Dutch oven over medium-high heat, warm 2 tablespoons olive oil. When hot, add the beef in batches and sear on all sides, about 2 minutes per side, adding more oil as necessary to prevent sticking. As you work, transfer the seared beef to a plate.

Reduce the heat to medium-low. If needed, add a bit more olive oil to the pot. Add the onion, garlic, and carrots, and cook, stirring occasionally until they start to soften, about 3 minutes.

Add the red wine, stirring with a wooden spoon to scrape up any browned bits from the pan bottom. Stir in the tomato paste and beef broth until well blended. Add the potatoes, thyme, oregano, and Worcestershire sauce, then return the beef to the pot.

Increase the heat to medium-high and bring the mixture to a simmer, then reduce the heat to low. Cover with the lid slightly ajar to allow steam to escape and simmer until the beef and potatoes are tender, 1½ to 2 hours.

Serve hot, accompanied by the bread of your choice.

Cottage Comfort
Chicken and Stars Soup

In a moment of shock and revelation, Feyre retreats to Rhysand's cottage, grappling with the newfound knowledge of their bond. As Rhysand shares the weighty tales of his past and explains the significance of the mating bond, the humble can of soup Feyre is heating on the stove turns into something more—an offering and silent acknowledgment. While we don't know the exact soup, Chicken and Stars is a classic canned soup favorite, and the little pasta stars are just too perfect for celebrating our favorite Night Court couple.

2½ pounds bone-in, skin-on chicken thighs

½ teaspoon Kosher salt, plus more for seasoning

Freshly cracked black pepper, to taste

2 tablespoons salted butter, plus more as needed

1 small yellow onion, diced

2 carrots, peeled and diced

2 stalks celery, diced

3 garlic cloves, minced

8 cups chicken broth

1 cup pastina (small star-shaped dry pasta)

¼ cup chopped fresh flat-leaf parsley leaves

2 tablespoons chopped fresh dill

Juice of ½ lemon, or more to taste

Sopping Up Crusty Bread (page 85), for serving

Season the chicken thighs generously with salt and pepper. In a large stockpot, melt 2 tablespoons butter over medium heat. Add the chicken thighs and cook until browned on all sides, 2 to 3 minutes per side, and transfer them to a plate. Do this in batches, if necessary, to avoid overcrowding.

Reduce the heat to medium-low. Add more butter to the stockpot if needed, 1 tablespoon at a time. Add the onion, carrots, celery, and garlic, along with ½ teaspoon of salt. Sauté, stirring occasionally, until the vegetables have softened, 2 to 3 minutes.

Add the broth and the browned chicken thighs back to the stockpot. Increase the heat to medium-high and bring the mixture to a simmer. Reduce the heat to medium-low, cover the pot with a lid, and simmer until the chicken thighs are cooked through, about 20 minutes.

Remove the chicken thighs from the soup and place them on a cutting board. Bring the soup to a boil over medium-high heat and add the pastina. Cook according to the package directions for al dente pasta.

While the pasta is cooking, use a sharp paring knife to remove and discard the skin and bones from the chicken. Chop the cooked chicken meat into 1-inch pieces. Set aside.

Once the pasta is cooked, add the chopped chicken, parsley, dill, and lemon juice to the pot. Taste and adjust the seasoning with additional salt, pepper, and lemon juice as desired.

Serve hot, accompanied by the bread.

ADVICE FROM ALIS

Should the star-shaped pasta known as pastina prove elusive in the shops, fret not, for it's easily found online, or you might just as well substitute it with another petite pasta shape, like orzo, Dear.

THE HOUSE'S HEARTY
PORK AND BEAN STEW

When Nesta sought a moment of respite after a long day working in the library, a steaming bowl of spicy pork and bean stew appeared, seemingly out of thin air. Inspired by Nesta's determination and The House's care in *A Court of Silver Flames*, indulge in this bewitching dish that combines warmth, spice, and a touch of magic.

3 to 4 pounds boneless pork shoulder or Boston butt, trimmed of excess fat and cut into 2-inch cubes

Kosher salt

Freshly cracked black pepper

2 tablespoons olive oil, plus more if needed

½ yellow onion, finely diced

2 carrots, peeled and diced

4 cloves garlic, minced

¼ cup harissa paste

¼ cup tomato paste

2 tablespoons light brown sugar

¼ cup red wine vinegar

8 cups chicken broth

2 (15-ounce) cans cannellini beans, drained and rinsed

1 bunch kale, stems removed, leaves torn into 1-inch pieces

Juice of 1 lemon

¼ cup chopped fresh cilantro, for garnish

Season the cubed pork shoulder generously with salt and pepper.

In a large Dutch oven or stockpot, warm the olive oil over medium heat. In batches to avoid overcrowding, add the cubed pork shoulder and cook until all sides are browned, 1 to 2 minutes per side. Transfer the seared pork to a large plate to catch any juices.

In the same pot, add the onion, carrots, and garlic. Sauté until the vegetables just begin to soften, 3 to 5 minutes, adding additional olive oil if needed.

Stir in the harissa paste, tomato paste, brown sugar, and red wine vinegar. Cook, stirring, for about 1 minute, ensuring that the vegetables are evenly coated.

Return the seared pork to the pot and stir to combine. Pour in the chicken broth, then reduce the heat to medium-low and simmer for 1 hour.

Add the drained cannellini beans, torn kale leaves, and lemon juice. Stir well, then let the stew simmer until the pork is tender and flavors meld together, about 30 more minutes.

To serve, ladle the stew into bowls and garnish with a sprinkle of chopped cilantro.

ADVICE FROM ALIS

If you're fixin' to whip up this dish in a slow cooker, start by givin' that well-seasoned pork shoulder a good sear, just like it says, in a cast iron skillet. After that, toss everything in the slow cooker except for them beans, kale, lemon, and cilantro. Let the pork simmer away on low for about 6 hours, then toss in the beans, kale, and a squeeze of lemon. Give it all a good stir and let it simmer low and slow for another 1 to 2 hours. Serve it up just like the recipe tells ya, Love.

STARLIT STUFFED CHICKEN WITH BERRY REDUCTION

This dish is inspired by the starlit skies of Velaris and little Nyx, a legend born from light and shadows. Chicken breasts are stuffed with a rich blend of ricotta, lemon zest, and fresh greens. To complement the filling, a berry reduction echoes the color of Nyx's deep blue eyes. The final touch of puff pastry stars reminds us of the court he was born to, making each plate a celebration of the Night Court's newest dawn.

1 sheet puff pastry, at room temperature

1 egg

Kosher salt

4 ounces ricotta cheese

Finely grated zest of 1 lemon

2 tablespoons chopped fresh flat leaf parsley

½ cup finely chopped fresh or frozen and thawed spinach

4 boneless, skinless chicken breasts

Freshly cracked black pepper

Olive oil

½ cup fresh or frozen blueberries

½ cup fresh or frozen blackberries

¼ cup sugar

1 tablespoon fresh lemon juice (from about ½ lemon)

Preheat the oven to 425ºF and line a baking sheet with parchment paper.

Unfold the puff pastry, if necessary, and place it flat on a work surface. Using a small, star-shaped cookie cutter, cut out 20 to 24 stars from the puff pastry sheet and place them on the prepared baking sheet. Whisk the egg in a small bowl. Brush the puff pastry stars with the egg wash and lightly sprinkle with salt. Bake the stars until golden brown, 5 to 8 minutes, then set aside to cool.

Reduce the oven temperature to 375ºF and line another baking sheet with aluminum foil.

In a bowl, combine the ricotta, lemon zest, parsley, and spinach. Mix well and set aside.

Place the chicken breasts on a cutting board between 2 layers of plastic wrap. Pound them to an even thickness of about ½ inch. Season both sides with salt and pepper.

Dollop ¼ of the ricotta mixture onto each chicken breast and spread evenly to coat the top of the chicken breasts, leaving ½ inch along the edges. Roll up the chicken breasts and secure with toothpicks if necessary. Brush the outside of each roll with olive oil.

Place the chicken rolls on the prepared baking sheet. Bake until the chicken is cooked through, and the filling is bubbly, 20 to 25 minutes.

While the chicken bakes, make the berry reduction: In a saucepan, combine the blueberries, blackberries, sugar, and lemon juice and place over medium heat. Cook until the berries break down and the sauce thickens, 10 to 12 minutes. Strain the berry reduction into a bowl using a mesh strainer to remove the seeds. Set aside to cool.

To serve, divide the chicken rolls and drizzle each with the berry reduction. Garnish with 4 or 5 puff pastry stars on each breast. Serve right away.

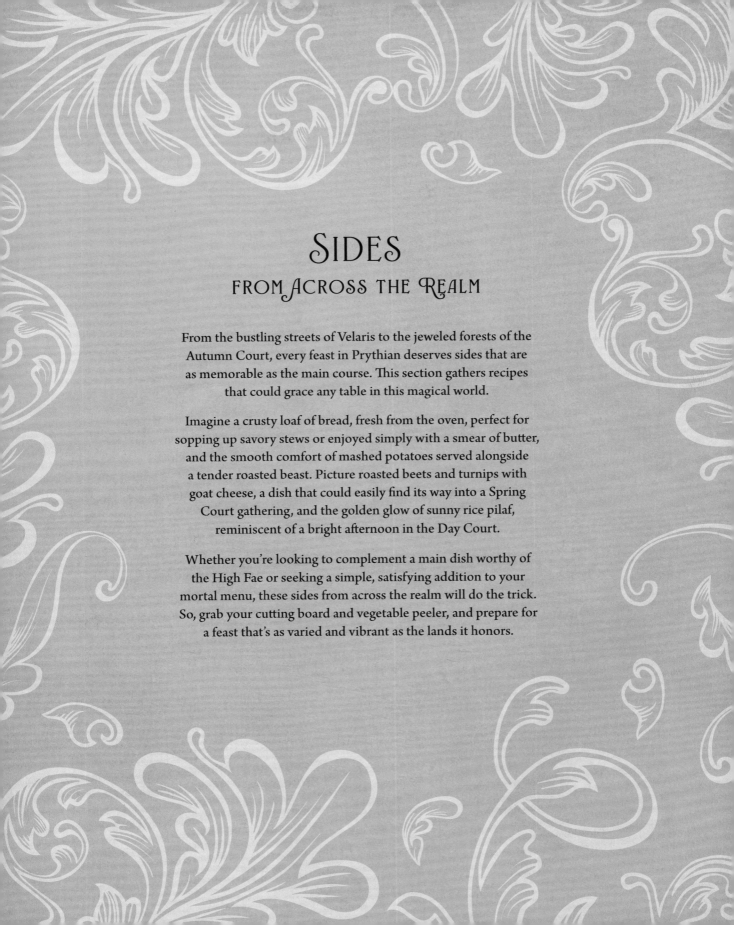

SIDES
FROM ACROSS THE REALM

From the bustling streets of Velaris to the jeweled forests of the Autumn Court, every feast in Prythian deserves sides that are as memorable as the main course. This section gathers recipes that could grace any table in this magical world.

Imagine a crusty loaf of bread, fresh from the oven, perfect for sopping up savory stews or enjoyed simply with a smear of butter, and the smooth comfort of mashed potatoes served alongside a tender roasted beast. Picture roasted beets and turnips with goat cheese, a dish that could easily find its way into a Spring Court gathering, and the golden glow of sunny rice pilaf, reminiscent of a bright afternoon in the Day Court.

Whether you're looking to complement a main dish worthy of the High Fae or seeking a simple, satisfying addition to your mortal menu, these sides from across the realm will do the trick. So, grab your cutting board and vegetable peeler, and prepare for a feast that's as varied and vibrant as the lands it honors.

SOPPING UP
CRUSTY BREAD

Every dinner table throughout the ACOTAR series seems to have a loaf of crusty bread on it, making this recipe a staple accompaniment to many of the recipes in this book. This bread is perfect for sopping up the last bits of Creamy Chicken and Wild Rice Soup (page 65) or for spreading with Roasted Bone Marrow Spread with Garlic and Parmesan (page 45). Add a savory twist to this bread by including the optional garlic powder and oregano or opt to keep it simple and straightforward.

3 teaspoons sugar

1 package (2¼ teaspoons) instant yeast

1⅓ cups warm water (about 100ºF)

1½ teaspoons kosher salt

2½ cups all-purpose flour

1½ teaspoons garlic powder (optional)

1 teaspoon dried oregano (optional)

In a large bowl, mix together the sugar and yeast. Pour the warm water over the mixture and let stand until the mixture is actively bubbling, about 3 minutes.

In a separate bowl, mix together the salt, flour, and, if using, garlic powder and oregano.

Add the flour mixture to the yeast mixture. Stir with a wooden spoon until it becomes too difficult, then knead with your hands to incorporate the remaining flour, until it is just combined. Cover the bowl with a clean kitchen towel and place it in a warm spot to rise until doubled in size, about 30 minutes.

Wet your fingers with cold water and gently detach the dough from the sides of the bowl. Perform a series of 4 folds by pulling up a side of the dough and folding it over the top. Cover the dough again with the towel and let it rise for an additional 30 minutes. Repeat the folding process once more.

Line a bowl with parchment paper. Shape the dough into a round loaf and place it on the parchment paper in the bowl. Cover it with the towel and let rise until doubled in size, about 30 minutes. Meanwhile, preheat the oven to 450ºF.

Place the Dutch oven in the oven with the lid on to preheat for 15 minutes. When the dough has risen, make 2 to 3 small cuts on top. Remove the top from the Dutch oven and carefully transfer the dough on the parchment paper to the Dutch oven. Replace the lid and bake the bread for 30 minutes, then remove the lid and bake until the bread is golden brown and crusty, 10 to 15 more minutes.

Transfer the bread to a clean cutting board and allow it to cool for 1 hour before slicing and serving.

PLOT TWIST
ROASTED ROOTS
WITH GOAT CHEESE

In the realm where epic feasts rival grand battles, these roasted beets and turnips steal the spotlight, turning humble root veggies into the night's unsung heroes. Goat cheese—the perfect partner in crime for beets—is added for a dash of tangy rebellion, turning each bite into a delicious little plot twist. So, whether you're dining in a grand hall or simply at your kitchen table, let this dish remind you that sometimes the boldest moves are made on the plate.

2 tablespoons olive oil, plus more for greasing

1 pound beets, trimmed, peeled, and cut into 1-inch dice

1 pound turnips, peeled and cut into 1-inch dice

½ red onion, sliced

6 cloves garlic, minced

1 tablespoon chopped fresh thyme

1 tablespoon chopped fresh rosemary

1 teaspoon kosher salt

¼ teaspoon freshly cracked black pepper

4 ounces soft goat cheese, crumbled

Preheat the oven to 400°F. Grease a rimmed baking sheet with olive oil.

Put the diced beets, turnips, sliced onion, and minced garlic on the prepared baking sheet. Drizzle with 2 tablespoons olive oil, then sprinkle with the chopped thyme, rosemary, salt, and pepper. Toss everything together until evenly coated and spread the ingredients out in an even layer. Roast in the preheated oven for 15 minutes. Remove the baking sheet from the oven, toss the vegetables, spread them out in an even layer, and return to the oven until the beets are tender and the turnips begin to turn golden, 10 to 15 minutes. Remove the baking sheet from the oven and allow the vegetables to cool for about 5 minutes.

Sprinkle the crumbled goat cheese over the warm vegetables. Serve warm.

ADVICE FROM ALIS

Don't hesitate to toss other root treasures onto the pan, such as sweet potatoes, red potatoes, carrots, or parsnips, Dear.

CARAMELIZED CARROTS
with HONEY and THYME

These caramelized carrots are inspired by the cozy lunch Nesta enjoyed at Emerie's shop in *A Court of Silver Flames* as they were getting to know one another. With just a hint of honey and a sprinkle of thyme, they're a simple yet delicious side dish for Rosemary and Garlic Roast Beef (page 67) or a sweet and savory accent for a casual dinner with friends.

1 pound carrots, peeled then cut in half first lengthwise then crosswise

¼ cup (½ stick) salted butter, melted

3 tablespoons honey

½ teaspoon chopped fresh thyme

½ teaspoon kosher salt, plus extra for sprinkling

¼ teaspoon freshly cracked black pepper

Preheat the oven to 425°F. Line a baking sheet with parchment paper or foil.

In a bowl, combine the carrots with the melted butter, 2 tablespoons of the honey, the thyme, salt, and pepper. Toss until the carrots are evenly coated.

Spread the carrots evenly on the prepared baking sheet. Place in the preheated oven and roast for 15 minutes.

Drizzle the carrots with the remaining 1 tablespoon honey and toss well. Continue to roast until the carrots are tender and slightly caramelized, about 10 minutes.

Remove the carrots from the oven, sprinkle with a little more kosher salt, and serve immediately.

THE UBIQUITOUS
GREEN BEANS OF PRYTHIAN

At this point, "green beans sautéed in garlic" might as well be the official side dish of Prythian—they're mentioned almost as often as "vulgar gestures." These green beans are straight out of the dinner spreads often found in the pages of ACOTAR, where they're a staple at lavish feasts and casual dinners alike. Roasted garlic adds a rich, aromatic touch, while a squeeze of lemon brings a needed zing. Simple to make, you'll find these green beans becoming a staple at your dinner table as well!

1 head garlic

2 tablespoons olive oil

1 pound green beans, trimmed

1 teaspoon kosher salt

½ lemon

Preheat the oven to 400°F. Cut off the top of the garlic head. Place the garlic head on a piece of foil, drizzle with 1 tablespoon olive oil, and wrap it in the foil. Roast in the preheated oven until the cloves are soft and fragrant, 30 to 45 minutes. Remove from the oven and set aside to cool.

Increase the oven heat to 425°F. Spread the green beans on a rimmed baking sheet. Toss them with the remaining 1 tablespoon olive oil and the salt. Roast in the preheated oven for 10 minutes. Toss the beans, spread them out again, and continue roasting until they have softened and browned slightly at the edges, 5 to 8 more minutes.

Squeeze the roasted garlic cloves out of their skins and onto the green beans. Squeeze the juice from the half lemon over the green beans. Toss everything together to evenly coat the beans. Taste and adjust the seasoning with additional salt if necessary. Serve warm.

Roasted VEGETABLE Medley with MAPLE BUTTER GLAZE

YIELDS

6

SERVINGS

Here's a dish that's sure to fuel you after a long day, just like one of Nesta's satisfying meals after a particularly trying ordeal. This medley of roasted sweet potatoes, brussels sprouts, and cauliflower is drizzled with balsamic vinegar and maple syrup, then sprinkled with fresh herbs. It's perfect alongside Townhouse Slow-Roasted Chicken with Sage and Lemon (page 64). Whether you're celebrating your own victories or just craving a warm, nutritious side dish, these buttery roasted veggies have you covered.

1 pound sweet potatoes,
peeled and cubed

1 pound brussels sprouts,
tough outer leaves
removed, halved

1 head cauliflower,
cut into florets

2 tablespoons
balsamic vinegar

1 tablespoon olive oil

1 tablespoon chopped
fresh rosemary

1 teaspoon chopped
fresh thyme

1 teaspoon kosher salt

2 tablespoons salted butter,
cut into thin slices

1 tablespoon pure
maple syrup

Preheat the oven to 400°F. Line a rimmed baking sheet with parchment paper.

In a large bowl, combine the sweet potatoes, brussels sprouts, and cauliflower florets. Drizzle with balsamic vinegar and olive oil. Add the chopped rosemary, thyme, and salt. Toss everything together until the vegetables are evenly coated. Spread the vegetables in a single layer on the prepared baking sheet. Roast in the preheated oven until the vegetables are tender and golden brown, 15 to 18 minutes.

While they are still hot, dot the vegetables with the butter and drizzle with maple syrup. Toss gently to coat, allowing the residual heat to melt the butter and blend the flavors. Serve immediately.

Sunny
Rice Pilaf

Inspired by the Day Court, this recipe is a tribute to the brilliance of Helion and his court. Saffron threads infuse basmati rice with a golden hue reminiscent of the sunlit lands, while toasted almonds and golden raisins add texture and sweetness. Crack open a good book in a sunny corner with a plate of this pilaf and imagine you're in one of the many libraries of the Day Court. This is delicious served with the Sevenda's Spiced Vegetarian Stew (page 71).

Pinch of saffron threads

¼ cup warm water

2 cups basmati rice

1 tablespoon ghee, plus more if needed

½ medium yellow onion, finely chopped

3 garlic cloves, minced

½ teaspoon ground coriander

1 teaspoon kosher salt

4 cups chicken or vegetable broth

½ cup golden raisins

⅓ cup toasted slivered almonds

Chopped fresh cilantro, for garnish

In a small bowl, soak the saffron threads in the warm water for about 10 minutes to bloom them.

Put the basmati rice in a sieve and rinse under cold water until the water runs clear. Drain off as much water as possible.

In a large saucepan or deep skillet, heat the ghee over medium heat. Add the onion and sauté until translucent and slightly golden, 3 to 5 minutes. Add the garlic and sauté until fragrant, about 1 minute. Add the rinsed basmati rice, salt, and coriander to the pot and stir to coat the rice. Sauté until the rice is slightly toasted, 3 to 5 minutes, adding additional ghee if necessary.

Pour in the chicken or vegetable broth and the saffron-infused water (including the saffron threads). Stir to mix.

Increase the heat to medium-high and bring the mixture to a gentle boil. Then, reduce the heat to low, cover the pot, and let it simmer until the rice is tender and the liquid is absorbed, about 15 minutes. Remove the pan from the heat and let stand, covered, for 5 minutes.

Fluff the rice with a fork. Stir in the golden raisins and toasted almonds. Taste and season with additional salt if desired. Sprinkle with chopped cilantro and serve warm.

Cheesy Chive
Mashed Potatoes

YIELDS
6-8
SERVINGS

These creamy herb-flecked potatoes pay homage to the comforting and hearty meals enjoyed throughout the series. By blending the richness of Boursin cheese and the freshness of chives, this dish makes a great side to many of the main dishes in this book, from Rosemary and Garlic Roast Beef (page 67) to Slow-Roasted Chicken with Sage and Lemon (page 64). Simple yet satisfying, this dish is a quiet nod to familiar comforts amidst tense conversations. We're thinking of you, Feyre, as you convince your sisters to let the Night Court use their home as a base in the Mortal Lands.

Kosher salt

2 pounds yellow potatoes, cut into 1-inch cubes

2 pounds russet potatoes, cut into 1-inch cubes

½ cup (1 stick) salted butter

4 cloves garlic, minced

1½ cups whole milk

1 package (5.2 ounces) shallot and chive Boursin cheese

1 tablespoon chopped fresh chives

½ teaspoon freshly cracked black pepper

In a stockpot, bring 3 quarts of water to a boil over high heat. Season the water with ¼ cup salt.

Carefully add the yellow and russet potatoes to the boiling water. Cook until the potatoes are fork-tender, 10 to 12 minutes. Drain the potatoes and set aside.

Add the butter to the empty stockpot and melt over medium-low heat. Add the garlic and sauté until fragrant and slightly golden, 1 to 2 minutes. Reduce the heat to low. Pour in the milk, then add the Boursin cheese to the pot and cook, stirring frequently, until the cheese is evenly melted and the mixture is smooth and blended. Turn off the heat.

Run the cooked potatoes through a potato ricer directly into the pot, then stir them with the milk-cheese mixture until blended. (Alternatively, return the potatoes to the pot and mash them using a potato masher, blending them with the milk-cheese mixture until smooth.)

Stir in the chives, ½ teaspoon kosher salt, and the pepper, stirring until just mixed. Be careful not to overmix, as it can make the potatoes gummy. Taste the mixture, adjusting the seasoning with additional salt if necessary, adding ½ teaspoon at a time and stirring and tasting after each addition. If needed, return the pot to medium-low heat, stirring the mashed potatoes until they are heated through.

Serve the mashed potatoes warm.

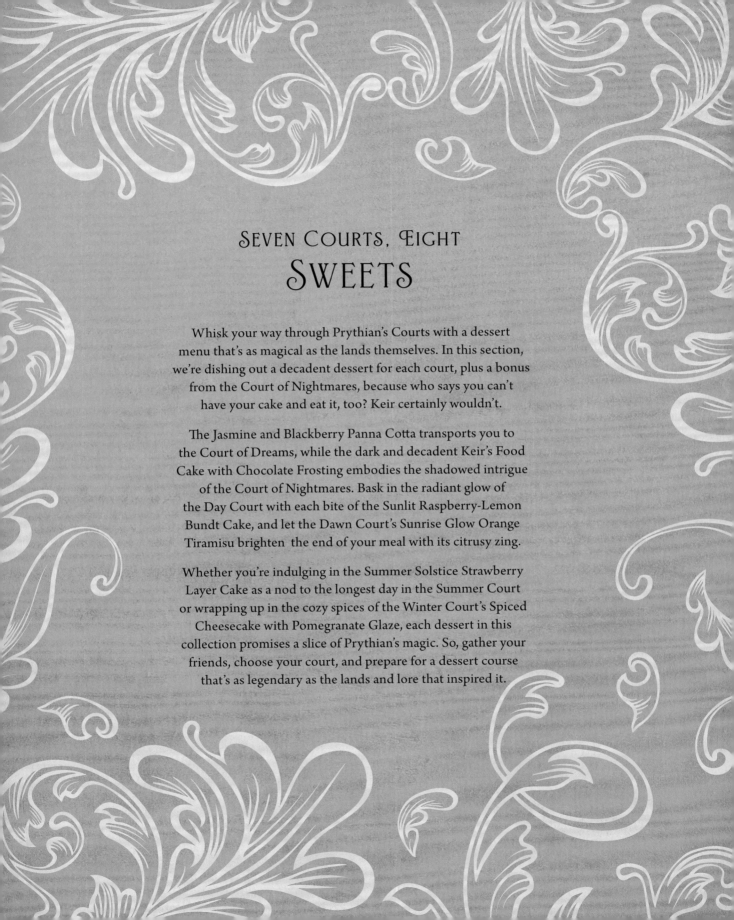

Seven Courts, Eight
Sweets

Whisk your way through Prythian's Courts with a dessert
menu that's as magical as the lands themselves. In this section,
we're dishing out a decadent dessert for each court, plus a bonus
from the Court of Nightmares, because who says you can't
have your cake and eat it, too? Keir certainly wouldn't.

The Jasmine and Blackberry Panna Cotta transports you to
the Court of Dreams, while the dark and decadent Keir's Food
Cake with Chocolate Frosting embodies the shadowed intrigue
of the Court of Nightmares. Bask in the radiant glow of
the Day Court with each bite of the Sunlit Raspberry-Lemon
Bundt Cake, and let the Dawn Court's Sunrise Glow Orange
Tiramisu brighten the end of your meal with its citrusy zing.

Whether you're indulging in the Summer Solstice Strawberry
Layer Cake as a nod to the longest day in the Summer Court
or wrapping up in the cozy spices of the Winter Court's Spiced
Cheesecake with Pomegranate Glaze, each dessert in this
collection promises a slice of Prythian's magic. So, gather your
friends, choose your court, and prepare for a dessert course
that's as legendary as the lands and lore that inspired it.

JASMINE AND BLACKBERRY PANNA COTTA

This dessert is like a little piece of the Night Court in a jar, combining smooth, creamy panna cotta with a hint of jasmine, which is reminiscent of walking through the starlit jasmine-scented streets of Velaris. The blackberry layer adds a touch of "night" to the dessert, lending a tart contrast to the creamy, mellow base. Welcome to the Night Court.

¼ cup blackberry jelly or seedless jam

2½ cups heavy cream

5 tea bags green jasmine tea

⅓ cup milk (skim, 1%, or 2%)

1 envelope (0.25 ounce) unflavored gelatin

½ cup sugar

1½ teaspoons pure vanilla extract

Fresh blackberries, for garnish

In a microwave-safe bowl, gently heat the blackberry jelly at 50% power in 30-second intervals, stirring after each interval, until melted. Divide the melted jelly among four, wide-mouth, 8-ounce mason jars. Refrigerate until the jelly sets, about 1 hour.

While the jelly is setting, prepare the panna cotta. In a saucepan, warm the cream over medium heat, stirring frequently, until the cream is just starting to bubble at the edges. Remove the cream from heat and add the tea bags. Steep for 15 minutes to infuse the cream with the tea.

Meanwhile, in a small bowl, combine the milk and gelatin, stirring until the gelatin is fully dissolved. Set aside.

Remove the tea bags from the cream. Stir in the sugar and return the saucepan to medium heat. Slowly bring the mixture to a boil, stirring constantly to prevent boiling over. Add the milk and gelatin mixture to the boiling cream, stirring until fully dissolved. Continue cooking and stirring for 1 minute. Remove the saucepan from heat and stir in the vanilla extract.

Allow the mixture to cool to room temperature, about 20 minutes.

Pour the cooled cream mixture over the set blackberry jelly in the mason jars.

Cover each jar with plastic wrap or place the lid onto each jar. Refrigerate until the cream layer is set, at least 4 hours, but ideally overnight.

Before serving, garnish each panna cotta with 2 to 3 fresh blackberries. Serve cold.

Summer Solstice
Strawberry Layer Cake

Welcome some summer energy into your life with a cake that captures the vibrant essence of a day in the Summer Court. It's like sunshine on a plate: bright, breezy, and impossible to resist. Imagine fresh strawberries with fluffy cream on layers of cake so light you'll think they've been kissed by Tarquin himself. It's perfect for those days when you're craving a slice of summer magic and a little courtly decadence. So, grab a fork and dive in—just be ready to fight off a water wraith for the last piece!

FOR THE CAKES

Nonstick cooking spray for greasing

2½ cups all-purpose flour

2 teaspoons baking powder

1 teaspoon baking soda

½ teaspoon kosher salt

1¾ cups granulated sugar

½ cup vegetable oil

2 large eggs, at room temperature

2 large egg whites, at room temperature

2 teaspoons pure vanilla extract

½ teaspoon pure almond extract

⅔ cup sour cream, at room temperature

¾ cup milk (any milk), at room temperature

To make the cakes, preheat the oven to 350°F. Grease three 8-inch round cake pans with cooking spray.

In a bowl, whisk together the flour, baking powder, baking soda, and salt. Set aside.

Using a stand mixer fitted with the paddle attachment, combine the granulated sugar, oil, eggs, egg whites, and extracts on medium speed until blended. Add the sour cream and mix until incorporated. With the mixer on low speed, gradually add the dry ingredients, mixing until just incorporated. On low speed, slowly add the milk, mixing until just blended. Scrape down the sides and bottom of the bowl as necessary. Do not overmix.

Divide the batter evenly among the prepared pans, tapping the pans on the countertop to remove any air bubbles.

Bake the cakes in the preheated oven until a toothpick inserted into the center of the cakes comes out clean, 18 to 22 minutes. Allow the cakes to cool in the pans on a wire rack for 20 minutes, then invert the cakes onto the rack to cool completely, about 1 hour.

FOR THE FILLING

½ cup granulated sugar

¼ cup water

*¼ cup fresh lemon juice
(from about 2 lemons)*

*4 cups fresh strawberries,
hulled
and quartered*

FOR THE FROSTING

*6 ounces cream cheese, at
room temperature*

⅔ cup powdered sugar

*⅔ teaspoon pure vanilla
extract*

*1½ cups very cold heavy
cream*

To make the filling, in a small saucepan, combine the sugar, water, and lemon juice over medium heat. Bring to a simmer, stirring constantly. Reduce heat to medium-low and simmer until thickened, 3 to 5 minutes. In a large bowl, toss the strawberries with the sugar mixture. Set aside.

To make the frosting, in the bowl of a stand mixer fitted with the whisk attachment, beat the cream cheese, powdered sugar, and vanilla extract until light and fluffy, 2 to 3 minutes. With the machine running, gradually pour in the heavy cream, increase the mixer to high speed, and whip until stiff peaks form, 2 to 3 minutes.

To assemble the cake, place 1 layer on a cake stand or platter. Using a spatula, spread one-third of the frosting over the cake, then top with one-third of the strawberry filling. Repeat with remaining layers, ending with a layer of strawberries.

Cut the cake into wedges and serve.

ADVICE FROM ALIS
Just a little forewarning, Dear—you'll be needing three 8-inch cake pans for this. Should you not have them at hand, disposable ones from the store will do just fine.

Sunlit
Raspberry–Lemon Bundt Cake

Whip up a slice of sunshine so bright, even the Day Court might pause their eternal scroll-keeping to sneak a taste. Zesty enough to rival Helion's wit and as refreshing as a sunny Day Court afternoon, this cake is your passport to the finer side of Prythian—no magical lineage required. So, don your finest white and gold, and let's get baking.

FOR THE BUNDT CAKE

Nonstick cooking spray for greasing

3 cups all-purpose flour

1 teaspoon baking soda

½ teaspoon baking powder

½ teaspoon kosher salt

1⅓ cups granulated sugar

½ cup (1 stick) unsalted butter, melted and cooled

½ cup vegetable oil

1 cup sour cream, at room temperature

3 large eggs, at room temperature

1½ tablespoons finely grated lemon zest (from about 2 lemons)

2 tablespoons fresh lemon juice (from about 1 lemon)

2 teaspoons pure vanilla extract

12 ounces fresh or frozen raspberries

FOR THE GLAZE

1½ cups powdered sugar, sifted

¼ cup (½ stick) salted butter, melted

2–3 tablespoons heavy cream

½ teaspoon pure vanilla extract

Preheat the oven to 350°F. Generously spray a Bundt pan with nonstick cooking spray and set aside.

In a large bowl, whisk together the flour, baking soda, baking powder, and salt. Set aside.

In the bowl of a stand mixer fitted with the paddle attachment, combine the granulated sugar, melted butter, vegetable oil, sour cream, eggs, lemon zest, lemon juice, and vanilla extract. Mix on medium speed until combined and creamy, 2 to 3 minutes.

With the mixer on low speed, gradually add the dry ingredients to the wet, mixing until just incorporated to avoid overmixing.

Stop the mixer. Using a rubber spatula, gently fold in the raspberries; the batter will be thick.

Transfer the batter to the prepared Bundt pan and smooth the top with the rubber spatula. Bake until a toothpick inserted into the cake comes out clean or with a few moist crumbs clinging to it, 45 to 60 minutes.

Allow the cake to cool in the pan on a wire rack for 20 minutes. Then, unmold the cake onto the rack to cool completely, about 1 hour.

To make the glaze, in a bowl, whisk together the powdered sugar, melted butter, 2 tablespoons cream, and vanilla until smooth and pourable. Adjust the consistency with additional heavy cream, if needed. Drizzle the glaze over the cooled cake. Let the glaze set, about 10 minutes.

Cut into slices to serve.

ADVICE FROM ALIS

This cake will stay delicious for a few days. Swaddle it in plastic wrap or cover it well, and let it rest in the refrigerator, Love.

Sunrise Glow
Orange Tiramisu

Kick-start your day (or night) with a slice of this twist on a traditional dessert, a tribute to the Dawn Court. It's as if you've scooped up a piece of the dawn sky—golden with the first light—and layered it with creamy, dreamy mascarpone. Infused with the zest of fresh oranges and layered between feather-light ladyfingers soaked in a mix of orange juice and Triple Sec, each bite bursts with sunny flavor. Topped with a silken orange curd that glows like Thesan himself, this dessert not only captivates the palate, but it isn't too hard on the eyes, either.

**FOR THE
ORANGE CURD**

*½ cup (1 stick) unsalted
butter*

4 large egg yolks

4 large eggs

¼ teaspoon kosher salt

1¼ cups sugar

Finely grated zest of 1 orange

*⅔ cup fresh orange juice
(from about 2 oranges)*

1½ cups cold heavy cream

*1 pound mascarpone cheese,
at room temperature*

*½ cup fresh orange juice
(from about 1 orange)*

*1 tablespoon triple sec
(optional)*

*Two packages (7 ounces
each) ladyfingers*

To make the orange curd, place the butter in a deep, heat-safe bowl. Set a fine mesh strainer over the bowl. In a heavy bottomed saucepan, whisk together the egg yolks, whole eggs, salt, sugar, orange zest, and orange juice. Cook over medium-low heat, whisking constantly, until the mixture comes to a simmer. Simmer for 1 minute, then remove from the heat. Strain the hot yolk mixture through a fine-mesh sieve into the bowl with the butter, pressing with a rubber spatula to smooth out any zest, pulp, and lumps. Stir until the butter melts and the mixture is smooth. Cover and refrigerate the curd until cold and thickened, about 30 minutes.

In the bowl of a stand mixer fitted with the whisk attachment, pour in the cream. Whisk on high speed until stiff peaks form, 2 to 3 minutes.

In a large bowl, whisk together half of the cooled orange curd and the mascarpone cheese until fully incorporated and smooth. Gently fold the whipped cream into the mascarpone mixture, being careful to maintain its fluffiness. This will become the filling. Cover and refrigerate the remaining orange curd until serving time.

To assemble, mix together the orange juice and triple sec (if using) in a wide, shallow bowl.

Continued

Have ready a 9-by-11-inch glass baking dish.

One at a time, briefly dip each ladyfinger into the orange juice mixture, then place them in tight rows inside the baking dish. When 1 layer of soaked ladyfingers has been formed, pour half of the filling over the top and spread it out to the edges. Repeat with another layer of ladyfingers and the remaining half of the filling, spreading it again to the edges. Cover and refrigerate for 8 hours or overnight.

Before serving, spread the remaining orange curd over the top of the tiramisu. Cut the tiramisu into squares and serve with a spatula.

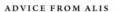

ADVICE FROM ALIS
This recipe calls for a fair share of cooling and setting, so it's wise to ready it the day prior to when you aim to serve it. In truth, it even tastes more delightful on the second day, Dear.

KEIR'S FOOD CAKE WITH CHOCOLATE FROSTING

In the shadowed depths of the Hewn City, where whispers of darkness echo off the stone, this cake would reign supreme. This devilish dessert, as dark and rich as the Court of Nightmares itself, offers a taste of indulgence in a realm where pleasure and power intertwine. Each slice is a decadent dance of bitter cocoa-laced cake layers and sweet chocolate buttercream. Just as Keir presides with heartless grace, this cake commands attention on any table. So, dare to take a bite, and let the flavors transport you to a celebration that's as sumptuous as it is sinister.

FOR THE KEIR'S FOOD CAKE

Nonstick cooking spray, for greasing

2¼ cups all-purpose flour

1 cup unsweetened cocoa powder

2 teaspoons baking soda

1 teaspoon baking powder

1 teaspoon kosher salt

⅓ cup vegetable oil

1 cup sour cream, at room temperature

½ cup (1 stick) unsalted butter, at room temperature

2 cups granulated sugar

½ cup light brown sugar, firmly packed

3 large eggs, at room temperature

2 teaspoons pure vanilla extract

1 cup freshly brewed hot coffee

Preheat the oven to 350ºF. Grease two 9-inch round cake pans with nonstick cooking spray.

In a large bowl, whisk together the flour, cocoa powder, baking soda, baking powder, and salt. In a separate bowl, whisk together the oil and sour cream. Set both aside.

Using a stand mixer fitted with the paddle attachment, beat the butter on medium speed until smooth, about 1 minute. Gradually add the granulated sugar and brown sugar, beating well after each addition and scraping down the sides and bottom of the bowl as necessary. Once all the sugar has been incorporated, increase the speed to high and beat until light and fluffy, about 4 minutes. Add the eggs one at a time, beating well after each addition. Add the vanilla extract and mix until blended.

With the mixer on the lowest speed, add the flour mixture in 3 additions, alternating with the sour cream mixture in 2 additions. Beat until just incorporated after each addition. Do not overmix. Stop the mixer and gently fold in the hot coffee with a spatula until just incorporated.

Divide the batter evenly between the prepared pans, smoothing the tops with a spatula.

Bake until a toothpick inserted into the center comes out clean or with a few moist crumbs attached, 35 to 45 minutes.

Cool the cakes in the pans on a wire rack for 20 minutes, then unmold them onto the rack to cool completely, about 1 hour.

**FOR THE
CHOCOLATE FROSTING**

*1½ cups (3 sticks) unsalted butter,
at room temperature*

5¼ cups powdered sugar

¾ cup unsweetened cocoa powder

*6 tablespoons milk, plus more if
needed*

Pinch of kosher salt

3 teaspoons pure vanilla extract

To make the chocolate frosting, in a stand mixer fitted with the paddle or whisk attachment, beat the butter on medium speed until light and creamy, about 3 minutes. In a bowl, sift together the powdered sugar and cocoa powder. Add the cocoa-sugar mixture, the milk, salt, and vanilla extract to the mixer. Start the mixer on low speed and mix for 30 seconds. Then, increase the mixer speed to high and beat until the frosting is light and fluffy, 1 to 2 minutes. Add additional milk if necessary to reach the desired consistency.

To assemble the cake, place 1 layer on a cake stand or plate. Using a spatula, spread a generous layer of frosting over the top of the cake layer. Place the second cake layer on top of the first, lining up the edges and apply frosting to the top and sides of the cake.

Cut the cake into slices and serve.

Chocolate Torte
with Mint Whipped Cream
and Fresh Raspberries

YIELDS
8
SERVINGS

Indulge in a slice (or two) of this chocolate torte, a dessert so magically decadent, it might just disappear right off your plate. Inspired by Feyre's first taste of true luxury at the Spring Court, this torte is a delicious rebellion in every bite. Rich, dark chocolate meets a hint of creamy mint and tart raspberries, creating a dessert so tempting, even the High Fae would pause to savor each bite. Go ahead, defy Tamlin's warning, and savor the richness.

FOR THE CHOCOLATE TORTE

Nonstick cooking spray, for greasing

9 ounces good-quality dark chocolate (65% cacao or higher), finely chopped

1 cup (2 sticks) plus 2 tablespoons unsalted butter

1½ cups sugar

7 large eggs, at room temperature

1 teaspoon pure vanilla extract

FOR THE MINT WHIPPED CREAM

3 tablespoons sugar

10 fresh mint leaves

1½ cups cold heavy cream

Fresh raspberries, for serving

Preheat the oven to 375ºF. Grease a 9-inch springform pan with nonstick cooking spray, line the bottom with parchment paper, and spray again.

Bring 2 inches of water to a simmer in a saucepan. Place a large heat-safe bowl over the pot. Add the chocolate and butter to the bowl and warm, stirring frequently, until both are completely melted. Remove the bowl from the pan and place on a work surface. Stir in the sugar and let the mixture stand for 5 minutes to cool.

Add the eggs to the chocolate mixture 1 at a time and whisk, fully incorporating each egg before adding the next. After all of the eggs have been added, continue to whisk until the batter is thick and glossy. Stir in the vanilla extract.

Pour the chocolate mixture into the prepared pan. Bake until the torte jiggles slightly in the center, 30 to 35 minutes. Do not overbake. Allow the cake to cool in the pan for at least 10 minutes before removing the springform rim. Transfer to a cake stand or platter.

To make the mint whipped cream, process the sugar and mint leaves in a food processor or mortar and pestle until the mint is finely ground with the sugar. In the bowl of a stand mixer fitted with a whisk attachment, whip the heavy cream and mint-sugar on medium-high speed until stiff peaks form, 3 to 4 minutes.

To serve, cut the torte into slices and top each slice with a generous dollop of mint whipped cream and several fresh raspberries.

Spiced Cheesecake with Pomegranate Glaze

Welcome to the Winter Court, where ice-crowned High Fae and enchanting snowscapes await. This cheesecake, like the court itself, is a masterpiece of chill and charm. Creamy, deliciously spiced, and crowned with a ruby-red pomegranate glaze, it's a dessert worthy of High Lord Kallias himself. Serve yourself a slice and let the magic of the Winter Court envelop your taste buds.

FOR THE GRAHAM CRACKER CRUST

1½ cups graham cracker crumbs (from about 12 full sheets graham crackers)

¼ cup sugar

5 tablespoons unsalted butter, melted

FOR THE CHEESECAKE

Four 8-ounce packages full-fat brick cream cheese, at room temperature

1 cup sugar

1 cup sour cream, at room temperature

1 teaspoon pure vanilla extract

1 teaspoon ground cinnamon

½ teaspoon ground nutmeg

½ teaspoon ground cloves

½ teaspoon ground ginger

3 large eggs, at room temperature

Adjust the oven rack to the lower-middle position and preheat the oven to 350ºF. Place a large piece of aluminum foil on the counter near the oven.

To make the crust, in a bowl, combine the graham cracker crumbs and sugar. Mix in the melted butter until the mixture is sandy. Press the mixture into the bottom and slightly up the sides of an ungreased 9- or 10-inch springform pan. Bake the crust in the preheated oven for 10 minutes. Remove and place the hot pan on the piece of foil on the counter.

To make the cheesecake, in a stand mixer fitted with a paddle attachment, combine the cream cheese and sugar. Beat on medium-high speed until smooth and creamy, about 2 minutes. Add the sour cream, vanilla extract, cinnamon, nutmeg, cloves, and ginger, and mix until incorporated. Add the eggs 1 at a time and mix on medium speed just until incorporated. Avoid overmixing.

Pour the cheesecake batter over the crust and smooth the top. Wrap the piece of aluminum foil around the springform pan. Place the wrapped pan inside a large roasting pan or rimmed baking sheet. Fill a teakettle with water and bring it to a boil. Pour boiling water into the roasting pan or baking sheet until it is about 2 inches high to create a water bath.

Continued

FOR THE POMEGRANATE GLAZE

2 cups unsweetened pomegranate juice

½ cup sugar

Fresh mint leaves, for garnish

Carefully transfer the pan to the preheated oven and bake until the center of the cheesecake wobbles slightly when the pan is gently shaken, 55 to 70 minutes. If the cheesecake starts to brown too quickly, tent it with foil. Turn off the oven, open the door slightly, and let the cheesecake cool in the water bath in the turned-off oven for 1 hour.

Remove the cheesecake from the oven and water bath. Let cool completely at room temperature, then cover with plastic wrap and refrigerate for at least 4 hours, or overnight.

To make the glaze, in a saucepan over medium heat, whisk together the pomegranate juice and sugar. Bring to a boil, reduce heat to low, and simmer uncovered until the juice has reduced by about half and thickened, about 30 minutes. Let cool, then refrigerate in an airtight container.

To serve, pour the pomegranate glaze over the cheesecake and spread with a spatula. It should form a layer about ¼ inch thick. Loosen the edge of cheesecake from the springform pan with a knife and remove the outer ring. Garnish the cake with mint leaves. For clean slices, dip the knife in warm water and wipe clean between cuts.

ADVICE FROM ALIS

This here cheesecake, Darlin', it's a real time-taker. You'll wanna start preppin', bakin', and lettin' it set at least a good day before you plan on servin' it up.

Peach Upside-Down Layer Cake
with Cream Cheese Frosting

YIELDS
8-10
SERVINGS

Whip up a slice of the Autumn Court with this cake, a dessert as dazzling as the court's jeweled forests. With a caramelized peach topping, each layer mirrors the oranges, golds, and browns of the autumn landscape, while the spiced cream cheese frosting adds a delightful richness. Beron himself would even approve! This cake is perfect for a feast in a court known for its cutthroat beauty, where every bite brings a blend of richness and warmth, just like an autumn day.

FOR THE TOPPING

¼ cup (½ stick) unsalted butter, cut into 4 pieces, plus extra for greasing

2 pounds sliced fresh or frozen peaches

⅔ cup firmly packed light brown sugar

2 teaspoons fresh lemon juice

FOR THE CAKE

2 cups all-purpose flour

2 tablespoons cornmeal

2 teaspoons baking powder

1 teaspoon kosher salt

1½ cups granulated sugar

½ cup firmly packed light brown sugar

4 large eggs

¾ cup (1½ sticks) unsalted butter, melted and slightly cooled

1 cup sour cream

1 teaspoon pure vanilla extract

Preheat the oven to 350°F. Butter the bottom and sides of two 9-inch round cake pans.

To make the topping, melt the butter in a large skillet over medium heat. Add the peaches and cook, stirring occasionally, until they begin to caramelize, 4 to 6 minutes. Stir in the brown sugar and lemon juice and cook until the sugar dissolves and the peaches are coated, about 2 minutes. Divide the peaches evenly between the prepared pans.

To make the cake, in a bowl, whisk together the flour, cornmeal, baking powder, and salt. Set aside.

In the bowl of a stand mixer fitted with the paddle attachment, combine the granulated sugar, brown sugar, and eggs. Mix on medium speed until thick and homogeneous, about 45 seconds. With the mixer running, gradually add in the melted butter, followed by the sour cream and vanilla extract, beating until incorporated. Reduce the mixer speed to low and gradually add in the flour mixture, mixing until just incorporated. Avoid overmixing. Divide the batter evenly between the two prepared pans, spreading it evenly over the fruit.

Bake the cakes in the preheated oven until a toothpick inserted into the center comes out clean, 35 to 40 minutes. Allow cakes to cool on a wire rack for 20 minutes.

Continued

FOR THE FROSTING

8 ounces cream cheese, at room temperature

½ cup (1 stick) unsalted butter, at room temperature

3 cups powdered sugar

1 teaspoon pure vanilla extract

¼ teaspoon kosher salt

½ teaspoon ground cinnamon

¼ teaspoon ground nutmeg

¼ teaspoon ground allspice

Milk, any type (optional, as needed)

To make the frosting, in the bowl of a stand mixer fitted with the whisk attachment, beat the cream cheese and butter on medium-high speed until smooth and fluffy, 2 to 3 minutes. Stop the mixer and add the powdered sugar, vanilla extract, salt, cinnamon, nutmeg, and allspice. Start the mixer on low speed, then increase to high speed, beating until smooth and fluffy, about 3 minutes. If needed, thin the frosting with milk, 1 tablespoon at a time, to reach the desired consistency.

Once the cakes have cooled, run a paring knife around the edges to loosen them from the pans. Invert each cake onto a cake stand or plate. Use the knife to replace any fruit that sticks to the pan. Using a spatula, spread a generous layer of frosting over the top of one cake layer, on top of the fruit. Place the second cake layer on top, lining up the sides, and spread the remaining frosting over the top and sides of the cake.

Using a long, sharp knife, cut the cake into 8 to 10 slices and serve.

Magical Morsels

Whip out your stand mixer and preheat those ovens; we're venturing into a realm where small bites deliver big magic. These recipes are a collection of bite-size delights that have danced through the pages of our favorite tales, each one an echo of a memorable moment. From Alis's comforting Molten Chocolate to the mischievously named Cassian's Banned Chocolate Cupcakes, these treats are more than just dessert—they're a gateway to the series' most heartwarming scenes.

Imagine nibbling on Midnight Chocolate Cookies while sneaking back to your room after a late-night snack. Or perhaps savoring a Caramel-Drizzled Apple Hand Pie as you gear up for a weekend of celebrations. Each recipe, from the Iced Heart-Shaped Cookies to the Not-So-Pathetic Biscuits, is a tribute to the moments that made us laugh and cry.

So, gather your fellow readers, a sprinkle of culinary magic, and a dash of creativity. It's time to transform your kitchen into a baker's haven where every stir is a nod to the epic saga we love.

Alis's
Molten Chocolate

Ever had one of those days where even a hot bath and a good book don't soothe your soul? That's when you need Alis's secret weapon: Molten Chocolate. It's like a hug in a mug! This recipe is straight from those moments in the Spring Court when only chocolate could make things better. Rich, indulgent, and easy to make, it's perfect for nights when you need a little extra comfort. So, whip up a cup, kick back, and let the chocolate do its job.

¼ cup heavy cream

1 teaspoon cornstarch

2 tablespoons powdered sugar

1 tablespoon unsweetened cocoa powder

¾ cup milk (2% or whole milk)

1.8 ounces good quality dark chocolate (70–75% cacao) chopped into small pieces

FOR THE WHIPPED CREAM

2 cups heavy cream

1 cup powdered sugar

1 teaspoon pure vanilla extract

In a small bowl, whisk together the heavy whipping cream and cornstarch until smooth.

In a separate small bowl, sift the cocoa powder and powdered sugar together.

In a small saucepan over medium heat, warm the milk, whisking constantly, until it comes to a simmer. Reduce the heat to low. Gradually whisk in the heavy cream–cornstarch mixture. Then, slowly add the cocoa powder–powdered sugar mixture, whisking until smooth. Add the chopped dark chocolate, continuing to whisk until the chocolate has fully melted and the mixture is well incorporated, about 3 to 5 minutes.

To make the whipped cream, using the clean bowl of the stand mixer or a large bowl with a handheld mixer, beat the heavy cream with the powdered sugar and vanilla extract on high speed until stiff peaks form, 3 to 4 minutes.

Serve immediately, topped with whipped cream.

ADVICE FROM ALIS

If you're craving a sweeter twist on my renowned Molten Chocolate, trade the dark chocolate for some high-quality milk chocolate, Darling.

Midnight
Chocolate Cookies

These cookies were made for midnight baking, just like when Feyre sought solace in the kitchens of the Spring Court. Imagine sneaking a cookie from the kitchen after a long day, then wandering back through the shadowed hallways as you ponder the day's events . . . or perhaps encounter someone unexpected. These cookies, soft and full of rich chocolate bits, are a nod to Feyre's midnight wandering while the rest of the Spring Court was out celebrating Calanmai.

¾ cup (1½ sticks) unsalted butter, at room temperature

1 cup loosely packed brown sugar

¾ cup granulated sugar

1 large egg

1 teaspoon pure vanilla extract

1½ cups all-purpose flour

½ cup unsweetened dark cocoa powder

1 tablespoon instant espresso powder (optional)

1 teaspoon baking soda

½ teaspoon kosher salt

¾ cup mini semisweet chocolate chips

Preheat the oven to 350°F. Line 2 baking sheets with parchment paper.

In the bowl of a stand mixer fitted with the paddle attachment, combine the butter, brown sugar, and granulated sugar. Mix on medium-high speed until fluffy and light, about 3 minutes. Add the egg and vanilla extract and continue to beat until fluffy and incorporated, about 2 minutes.

In a separate large bowl, whisk together the all-purpose flour, dark cocoa powder, espresso powder (if using), baking soda, and salt. With the mixer on low speed, gradually add the dry ingredients to the butter-sugar-egg mixture, mixing until just incorporated. Stop the mixer and stir in the chocolate chips until just incorporated. Do not overmix.

Using about 3 tablespoons per cookie, form the dough into balls and place them about 2 inches apart on the prepared cookie sheets. Bake in the preheated oven until just set, 8 to 10 minutes.

Remove the cookies from the oven and allow them to rest on the baking sheets for 10 minutes. These cookies are best enjoyed warm.

ICED
HEART-SHAPED COOKIES

In the spirit of Solstice, where family and feasting come together, these cookies are a nod to Feyre's sweet moments in the kitchen with Elain. Forget the endless pile of work that will still be there after the celebrations. Now it's time for sugar-frosted treats that look as enchanting as they taste. With a recipe inspired by sisterly love and the magic of the holidays, these cookies are your invitation to ditch the paperwork and dive into the joy of baking. So, don an apron over your finest gown and let every sprinkle of sugar be a reminder: Solstice is for savoring the sweet things in life.

FOR THE COOKIES

1 cup granulated sugar

¾ cup (1½ sticks) unsalted butter, softened

2 large eggs

½ teaspoon pure vanilla extract

2½ cups all-purpose flour

1 teaspoon baking powder

½ teaspoon kosher salt

To make the cookies, in the bowl of a stand mixer fitted with the paddle attachment, beat the sugar and butter on medium-high speed until light and fluffy, 2 to 3 minutes. Add the eggs 1 at a time, beating well after each addition. Mix in the vanilla extract.

In a separate bowl, whisk together the flour, baking powder, and salt. With the mixer set to low, gradually add the flour mixture, mixing just until incorporated. Do not overmix.

Divide the dough into 2 portions, wrap each in plastic wrap, and refrigerate for at least 1 hour, or up to overnight.

Preheat the oven to 400°F. Line 2 baking sheets with parchment paper.

On a lightly floured surface, use a rolling pin to roll out the dough to an even thickness of ¼ to ½ inch. Using a 3-inch heart-shaped cookie cutter, cut out as many shapes as you can. Gather the scraps, re-roll, and continue cutting out cookies until as much of the dough is used as possible. If the dough becomes too soft, refrigerate it again before continuing.

Place the cookies on the prepared baking sheets, spacing them about ½ inch apart. Bake until the cookies are lightly browned around the edges, 6 to 8 minutes. Transfer the cookies to a wire rack to cool completely.

Continued

FOR THE ICING

3 cups powdered sugar, sifted

*About ⅓ cup water,
at room temperature*

2 teaspoons light corn syrup

*½ teaspoon pure
vanilla extract*

Pink food coloring

To make the icing, in a bowl, whisk together the powdered sugar, ¼ cup water, corn syrup, and vanilla extract. Gradually whisk in additional water, 1 tablespoon at a time, until the icing reaches a consistency such that a ribbon of icing holds its shape for a few seconds before melting back into the bowl when drizzled from a whisk. Starting with 1 to 2 drops, add pink food coloring to the icing, stirring, and adding more until the desired color is achieved.

Transfer the icing to a squeeze bottle or piping bag fitted with a tiny tip. Outline the edges of the cooled cookies with icing first, then fill in the centers. Allow the icing to set completely before serving, which may take several hours.

ADVICE FROM ALIS
To hasten the setting of the icing, place the frosted cookies back on the baking tray and tuck it into the coolness of the refrigerator for an hour or two, Dear.

CARAMEL–DRIZZLED
APPLE HAND PIES

Step right into the heart of Solstice at the Night Court with these fruit-filled hand pies. Inspired by a kitchen bustling with the magic of Elain's baking, these pies are a bite-sized homage to the joy and warmth of family gatherings. Wrapped in flaky pastry and drizzled with homemade caramel, each spiced apple pie is a fusion of love and tradition. Perfect for sharing with your sisters or sneaking in a late-night treat with your High Lord. Bake, share, and devour, for Solstice is for family and feasting.

FOR THE HAND PIES

1 package puff pastry, at room temperature (2 sheets)

2 to 3 green apples, peeled, cored, and diced

⅓ cup firmly packed light brown sugar

2 teaspoons all-purpose flour, plus more for dusting the work surface

1 tablespoon fresh lemon juice (from about ½ lemon)

1 teaspoon ground cinnamon

½ teaspoon ground nutmeg

1 large egg, lightly beaten

FOR THE CARAMEL SAUCE

1 cup granulated sugar

6 tablespoons unsalted butter, at room temperature

½ cup heavy cream

½ teaspoon sea salt

Vanilla ice cream, for serving (optional)

Preheat the oven to 350°F.

In a large bowl, mix together the diced apples, brown sugar, 2 teaspoons flour, lemon juice, cinnamon, and nutmeg. Set aside.

Dust a work surface lightly with flour and place the pastry sheets flat on top. Using a large knife, cut each puff pastry sheet into nine 3x3 inch squares for a total of 18 squares.

Spoon about ¼ cup of the apple mixture into the center of 9 of the squares. Brush the edges with beaten egg. Top the filled squares with an unfilled pastry square, pressing the edges with a fork to crimp and seal them. Cut a 1-inch slit in the top of each pie.

Arrange the pies on an ungreased baking sheet and brush the tops with the remaining beaten egg. Bake the pies in the preheated oven until golden brown, 18 to 20 minutes.

To make the caramel sauce, in a heavy-bottomed saucepan, heat the granulated sugar over medium-low heat until melted and browned to an amber color, stirring frequently, about 5 to 7 minutes. Watch carefully to prevent burning. Once melted, remove the pan from the heat and stir in the butter. Add the heavy cream and sea salt, stirring until completely smooth. Be careful when adding the butter and cream; the mixture will bubble vigorously. Transfer the caramel sauce to a bowl or jar and allow to cool.

When the pies have finished baking, let cool on the baking sheet for about 10 minutes.

Serve the baked hand pies warm and drizzled with caramel sauce, accompanied by vanilla ice cream, if desired.

HAPPY BIRTHDAY, FEYRE!
CUPCAKES

Get ready to celebrate the birth of our favorite High Lady with a twist on the colossal pink cake described in *A Court of Silver Flames*. Perfect for a party, these cupcakes feature a classic birthday-cake base topped with a creamy strawberry frosting. The pink frosting not only looks gorgeous, but it also packs a flavor punch, making sure these cupcakes stand out amongst the other Winter Solstice fare for the birthday girl. So, whether you're honoring Feyre or just in the mood for a celebratory treat, these cupcakes are sure to add that extra sparkle to any occasion.

FOR THE CUPCAKES

2½ cups all-purpose flour

2 teaspoons baking powder

½ teaspoon baking soda

½ teaspoon kosher salt

¾ cup (1½ sticks) unsalted butter, at room temperature

1½ cups granulated sugar

3 eggs, at room temperature

1¼ cups sour cream, at room temperature

2 teaspoons pure vanilla extract

Preheat the oven to 350°F. Line two 12-cup standard cupcake pans with paper cupcake liners.

In a large bowl, mix together the flour, baking powder, baking soda, and salt.

In the bowl of a stand mixer fitted with the paddle attachment, cream the butter and sugar on high speed until light and fluffy, about 3 minutes.

Reduce the mixer speed to medium-low. Add the eggs one at a time, beating until fully incorporated before adding the next. Add the sour cream and vanilla and beat on low speed until incorporated, then increase to high speed and mix for about 1 minute.

Reduce the mixer speed to low and gradually add the flour mixture to the batter until just incorporated. Remove the bowl from the mixer and use a spatula to ensure the batter is thoroughly mixed.

Using a ¼ cup measuring cup, divide the batter evenly among the cupcake cups. Bake in the preheated oven until the cupcakes spring back when lightly pressed in the center, 16 to 20 minutes.

Remove the cupcakes from the oven and let cool in the pans for 10 minutes, then remove the cupcakes from the pans and transfer to a wire rack to cool completely.

Continued

*1 bag (2 ounces)
freeze-dried strawberries*

*1 cup (2 sticks) unsalted butter,
at room temperature*

4 cups powdered sugar

*¼ cup milk, at room
temperature (1%, 2%, or
whole), plus more if needed*

*1 teaspoon pure
vanilla extract*

To make the frosting, process the freeze-dried strawberries in a food processor or blender until they are a very fine powdery texture. Sift them through a fine-mesh sieve to remove any larger pieces and seeds.

In the bowl of a stand mixer fitted with the whisk attachment, beat the butter on medium-high speed until light and creamy, about 2 minutes. Add the powdered sugar, strawberry powder, milk, and vanilla. Start the mixer on low speed for 30 seconds, then gradually increase to high and beat until light and fluffy, about 3 minutes, stopping to scrape down the sides at least once. Adjust consistency with additional milk if needed.

Frost the cooled cupcakes with the strawberry frosting and serve.

ADVICE FROM ALIS

Though it might sound a tad unusual, freeze-dried strawberries should be lurking somewhere near other dried fruits in your grocery store, Dear, or, in a pinch, can be found online.

NOT-SO-PATHETIC
BISCUITS

Celebrate the moment Nesta finally embraces her bond with Cassian with these biscuits, inspired by their playful exchange in *A Court of Silver Flames.* Far from the original stale biscuit, these cookies are delicious, filled with sweet raspberry jam and featuring a heart-shaped cutout to symbolize their union. They're a delicious nod to Nesta's reluctant, yet heartfelt acceptance of their destined connection.

1 cup (2 sticks) unsalted butter,
at room temperature

⅔ cup sugar

1 teaspoon pure
vanilla extract

2 large eggs,
at room temperature

¼ teaspoon kosher salt

2½ cups all-purpose flour,
plus more for dusting

½ cup raspberry jam

In the bowl of a stand mixer fitted with the paddle attachment, cream the butter and sugar on medium-high speed until light and fluffy, about 2 minutes. Beat in the vanilla, then add the eggs one at a time, mixing well after each addition. Beat in the salt. With the mixer on low speed, gradually add the flour, ½ cup at a time, mixing until just incorporated. The dough will resemble large buttery crumbles.

Using your hands, gently press the dough together to form a cohesive ball. Divide the dough into two equal portions. Flatten each portion into a disk, wrap each disk in plastic wrap, and refrigerate for at least 30 minutes, or up to overnight.

Preheat the oven to 350ºF. Line 2 baking sheets with parchment paper.

Place 1 dough disk on a lightly floured surface, Using a rolling pin, roll out the dough until ¼ inch thick. Using a 2½-inch round cookie cutter dipped in flour, cut out as many shapes as you can. Transfer the rounds to the prepared baking sheets, spacing them ½ inch apart. Use a small heart-shaped cutter to cut a heart in the center of half of the dough round. Repeat with the remaining dough disk, re-rolling and cutting the scraps as necessary.

Bake the cookies in the preheated oven until the edges start to turn golden brown, but the tops remain pale, 12 to 15 minutes. Allow the cookies to cool on the baking sheet for 2 minutes, then use a spatula to transfer them to a wire rack to cool completely.

Once cooled, spread a thin layer of raspberry jam on the flat side of each solid biscuit. Top each with a heart cut-out biscuit, lining up the edges and pressing gently to form a sandwich.

PISTACHIO MINI CAKES
WITH WHIPPED CREAM
AND RASPBERRY DRIZZLE

Just as Emerie conjures a slice of pistachio cake from The House, you can summon that spellbinding charm into your own kitchen. These light and airy pistachio cupcakes are a tribute to that sleepover with Nesta, Gwyn, and Emerie. So, call out your wish for a sweet treat and let the magic happen as if The House itself were serving you.

FOR THE MINI CAKES

1½ cups shelled unsalted pistachios

2½ cups all-purpose flour

2 teaspoons baking powder

½ teaspoon baking soda

1 teaspoon kosher salt

¾ cup (1½ sticks) unsalted butter, at room temperature

1¾ cups granulated sugar

5 large egg whites, at room temperature

½ cup sour cream, at room temperature

2 teaspoons pure vanilla extract

1 teaspoon pure almond extract

1 cup whole milk, at room temperature

FOR THE RASPBERRY DRIZZLE

1 cup raspberry jam

2 tablespoons fresh lemon juice (from about 1 lemon)

FOR THE WHIPPED CREAM

2 cups heavy cream

1 cup powdered sugar

1 teaspoon pure vanilla extract

Preheat the oven to 350°F. Line two standard cupcake pans, and half of a third cupcake pan, with paper liners.

In a food processor, pulse the pistachios until finely ground. In a large bowl, combine the ground pistachios, flour, baking powder, baking soda, and salt. Set aside.

Using a stand mixer fitted with the whisk attachment or a handheld mixer, beat the butter and sugar on high speed until smooth and creamy, about 3 minutes. Scrape down the sides as necessary. Add the egg whites and continue to beat on high speed until fluffy and incorporated, about 2 minutes. On medium speed, add the sour cream, vanilla extract, and almond extract and mix until completely incorporated, about 1 minute.

With the mixer on low speed, slowly add the dry ingredients until just incorporated. Continue to mix on low speed, gradually adding the milk, until just incorporated.

Using a ¼ cup measuring cup, divide the batter evenly among the cupcake cups. Bake in the preheated oven until a toothpick inserted into the center of a cupcake comes out clean, 18 to 20 minutes.

Remove the cupcakes from the oven and let cool completely in the pans set on a wire rack.

To make the raspberry drizzle, in a small saucepan over medium-low heat, combine the raspberry jam and lemon juice. Cook, stirring occasionally, until thickened, about 5 minutes.

To make the whipped cream, using the clean bowl of the stand mixer or a large bowl with a handheld mixer, beat the heavy cream with the powdered sugar and vanilla extract on high speed until stiff peaks form, 3 to 4 minutes.

Serve the cupcakes topped with whipped cream and a trickle of raspberry drizzle.

CASSIAN'S BANNED

CHOCOLATE CUPCAKES

These cupcakes are the perfect treat when you're feeling a bit rebellious—or just hungry for something sinfully chocolatey. Inspired by Nesta's defiant indulgence in that double-chocolate cake served by The House in the face of Cassian's training plans, these cupcakes are as rich as they come. With an espresso-infused batter and decadent chocolate buttercream, each bite is a silent salute to doing what you shouldn't (according to Cassian, anyway). These are perfect for sharing with friends or keeping for yourself, because, let's face it, some rules are meant to be broken.

FOR THE CUPCAKES

1½ cups all-purpose flour

1 cup unsweetened cocoa powder

2 teaspoons instant espresso powder

1½ teaspoons baking powder

1 teaspoon baking soda

½ teaspoon kosher salt

1 cup granulated sugar

1 cup firmly packed light brown sugar

⅔ cup vegetable oil

2 teaspoons pure vanilla extract

4 large eggs, at room temperature

⅔ cup milk (any type), at room temperature

Preheat the oven to 350ºF. Line three standard 12-cup muffin pans with paper liners.

In a large bowl, whisk together the flour, cocoa powder, espresso powder, baking powder, baking soda, and salt. Set aside.

In the bowl of a stand mixer fitted with the paddle attachment, beat the granulated sugar, brown sugar, oil, and vanilla on medium speed until combined, about 2 minutes. Add the eggs one at a time and mix until fully incorporated before adding the next one. Gradually add the flour mixture, mixing until just incorporated. With the mixer on low speed, slowly add the milk, mixing until just incorporated. The batter will be thin.

Pour the batter into the prepared muffin pans, filling each cup halfway. Do not overfill. Bake in the preheated oven until a toothpick inserted into the center comes out clean, 18 to 20 minutes.

Remove the cupcakes from the oven and let cool in the pans on a wire rack for 10 minutes. Remove the cupcakes from the pans, place them directly on the rack, and let cool completely, 20 to 30 minutes.

FOR THE FROSTING

*1 cup (2 sticks) unsalted butter,
at room temperature*

*3½ cups powdered sugar,
plus more if needed*

½ cup unsweetened cocoa powder

*¼ cup milk (any type),
plus more if needed*

2 teaspoons pure vanilla extract

*Pinch of kosher salt,
plus more if needed*

Chocolate sprinkles, optional

To make the frosting, in a stand mixer fitted with the paddle or whisk attachment, beat the butter on medium speed until light and creamy, about 2 minutes. Add the powdered sugar, cocoa powder, milk, vanilla extract, and salt. Start the mixer on low speed for 30 seconds, then gradually increase to high and beat until lightened in color and fluffy, about 1 minute. Adjust the consistency if needed with additional powdered sugar for thickening or milk for thinning. Taste and adjust with an additional pinch of salt if desired.

Frost the cooled cupcakes and sprinkle with chocolate sprinkles, if using.

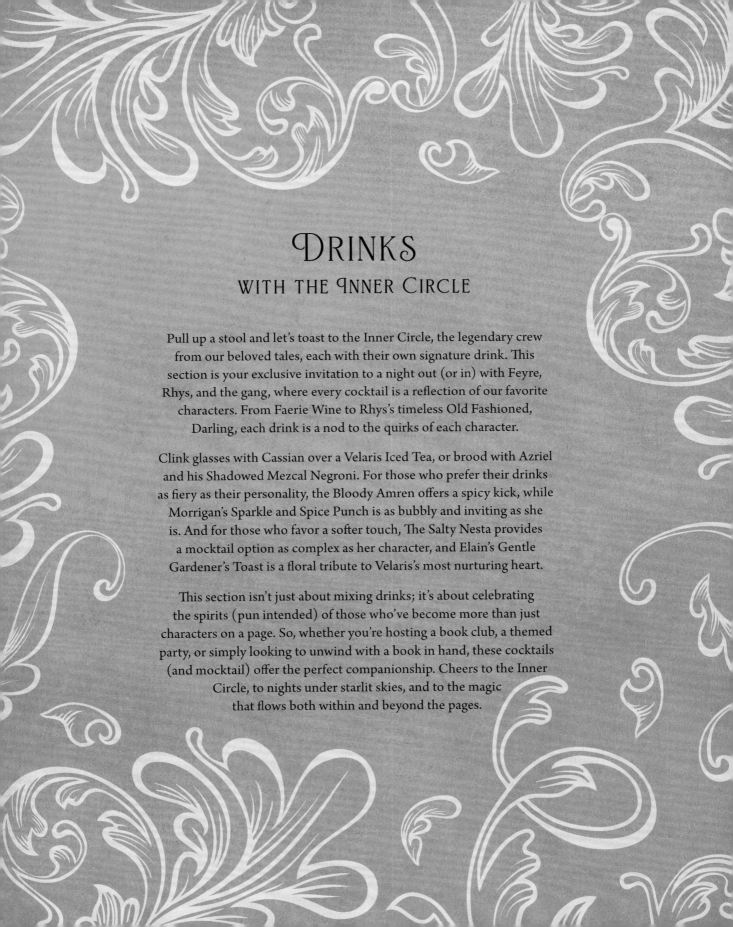

DRINKS
WITH THE INNER CIRCLE

Pull up a stool and let's toast to the Inner Circle, the legendary crew
from our beloved tales, each with their own signature drink. This
section is your exclusive invitation to a night out (or in) with Feyre,
Rhys, and the gang, where every cocktail is a reflection of our favorite
characters. From Faerie Wine to Rhys's timeless Old Fashioned,
Darling, each drink is a nod to the quirks of each character.

Clink glasses with Cassian over a Velaris Iced Tea, or brood with Azriel
and his Shadowed Mezcal Negroni. For those who prefer their drinks
as fiery as their personality, the Bloody Amren offers a spicy kick, while
Morrigan's Sparkle and Spice Punch is as bubbly and inviting as she
is. And for those who favor a softer touch, The Salty Nesta provides
a mocktail option as complex as her character, and Elain's Gentle
Gardener's Toast is a floral tribute to Velaris's most nurturing heart.

This section isn't just about mixing drinks; it's about celebrating
the spirits (pun intended) of those who've become more than just
characters on a page. So, whether you're hosting a book club, a themed
party, or simply looking to unwind with a book in hand, these cocktails
(and mocktail) offer the perfect companionship. Cheers to the Inner
Circle, to nights under starlit skies, and to the magic
that flows both within and beyond the pages.

FAERIE
WINE

Uncork the magic of Faerie Wine, a bewitching blend that promises euphoria with every sip. Inspired by Feyre's unforgettable nights of tipsy joy, this concoction is your ticket to dance under the stars like your favorite High Lady. Whether you're toasting a celebration or just looking to add a splash of enchantment to your evening, a glass of this spirited mix, complete with Prosecco and a medley of citrus and berries, will have you and your companions feeling like High Fae. Remember, though, it's all fun and games until you end up sloppily decorating for the Winter Solstice—just ask Feyre and Cassian.

1 cup orange-pineapple juice blend (or ½ cup orange juice and ½ cup pineapple juice)

½ cup white rum

¼ cup triple sec

¼ cup elderflower liqueur, such as St. Germain (optional)

2 tablespoons simple syrup

1 orange, thinly sliced

1 lime, thinly sliced

1 lemon, thinly sliced

1 pint fresh raspberries

1 bottle (750 ml) chilled Prosecco or your favorite sparkling white wine

Ice, for serving

In a large pitcher, combine the orange-pineapple juice, rum, triple sec, elderflower liqueur (if using), and simple syrup. Stir well.

Add the orange, lime, and lemon slices to the pitcher, along with the raspberries, reserving some of the fruit slices and raspberries for garnishing the glasses. Refrigerate the mixture until you're ready to serve, allowing the flavors to meld together.

Just before serving, gently pour the chilled Prosecco into the pitcher. Stir carefully to mix.

To serve, fill wineglasses halfway with ice. Pour the Faerie Wine over the ice. Garnish each glass with the reserved fruit slices and raspberries.

ADVICE FROM ALIS
Making a small batch of simple syrup is easy as plucking fruit from a tree. Just mix equal parts sugar and water in a saucepan, simmer until the sugar dissolves, then cool and store the mixture in a jar in the icebox. It's a sweet secret weapon for sprucing up drinks whenever you need it.

An Old Fashioned,
Darling

Raise a glass to Rhysand with a cocktail that's as smooth as the High Lord himself. It's a delicious spin on the classic Old Fashioned, mixing in blackberry and vanilla for a hint of Night Court vibes, then topped with a sprinkle of edible black glitter that's as captivating as a starry sky. Just like Rhys, it's a little unexpected and a lot delightful.

FOR THE BLACKBERRY-VANILLA SIMPLE SYRUP

½ cup sugar

½ cup water

½ cup fresh or frozen blackberries

1 vanilla bean, split lengthwise

Ice

3 dashes bitters

1 teaspoon water

2 ounces bourbon

½ teaspoon edible black glitter

Fresh blackberries, for garnish

Orange twist, for garnish

To make the blackberry-vanilla simple syrup, in a saucepan over medium heat, combine the sugar, water, blackberries, and vanilla bean. Cook, stirring and crushing the blackberries and vanilla bean with a wooden spoon until the sugar dissolves and the berries and vanilla release their flavors, 7 to 8 minutes. Remove from heat and let the mixture cool.

Strain the cooled syrup through a fine-mesh sieve to remove the solids and store in an airtight container in the refrigerator.

Fill a rocks glass with ice. Pour in ½ ounce Blackberry-Vanilla Simple Syrup (reserve the rest for another use) the bitters, water, and bourbon. Stir gently to combine the ingredients. Sprinkle the edible black glitter into the glass and stir lightly to lend a shimmering effect. Garnish the drink with a few fresh blackberries and an orange twist. Serve immediately.

Velaris
Iced Tea

Whip up a Velaris Iced Tea and channel your inner Cassian—our favorite charming, fiery warrior with a zest for life (and a bit of a mischievous streak). This isn't your standard Long Island Iced Tea; it calls for cinnamon whisky, which mirrors Cassian's iconic red siphons, and orange juice instead of lemon. It's the perfect drink for those nights when you're feeling a little rowdy or in need of extra courage to soar through the skies of Velaris.

Ice

2 ounces cinnamon whisky, such as Fireball

1 ounce vodka

1 ounce tequila

½ ounce triple sec

¾ ounce fresh orange juice

Cola, to top off

Orange wedge, for garnish

Fill a pint glass with ice. Pour the cinnamon whisky, vodka, tequila, triple sec, and freshly squeezed orange juice over the ice. Top off the glass with cola until nearly full. Stir the mixture gently to mix the ingredients well.

Garnish the glass with an orange wedge and serve immediately.

THE
SALTY NESTA

Sip on one of these refreshing drinks and embrace the fiery spirit of Nesta Archeron. This cocktail mirrors Nesta's own sharp nature, with a tangy edge of grapefruit that's as compelling as her character. Opt for the gin to add a kick or skip it if you're channeling sober Nesta. Either way, this drink, with its salty rim, is a fun homage to her famously tough exterior—no actual bark or bite included.

Kosher salt

1 lemon wedge

½ ounce fresh lemon juice

Ice for serving

4 ounces grapefruit soda, such as Squirt

2 ounces gin (optional)

Half grapefruit wheel, for garnish

Sprinkle a small amount of kosher salt onto a plate. Cut a slit in the center of the lemon wedge and rub it around the rim of a highball or large rocks glass. Dip the rim of the glass in the kosher salt to coat it.

Fill the salt-rimmed glass with ice cubes. Pour the lemon juice and grapefruit soda over the ice. If using gin, add 2 ounces to the glass. Stir gently.

Garnish the drink with a half wheel of grapefruit dropped into the glass. Serve immediately.

SHADOWED
MEZCAL NEGRONI

Raise a glass to the stoic Azriel with this cocktail, a drink as dark and intriguing as the Night Court's spymaster himself. Just like Azriel, this drink blends the unexpected—the smoke of mezcal, the bite of Campari, and a hint of sweetness, all shrouded in a veil of mystery thanks to the activated charcoal. It's the perfect sip for those nights when you're weaving shadows or just lounging with your own Inner Circle. So, channel your inner shadowsinger, embrace the night, and let this cocktail whisper its secrets with every delicious sip.

Ice for mixing, plus 1 large ice cube for serving

1½ ounces mezcal

1 ounce Campari

½ ounce sweet vermouth

½ teaspoon powdered activated charcoal (optional)

Orange half-wheel, for garnish

Fill a pint glass with ice. Add the mezcal, Campari, sweet vermouth, and activated charcoal (if using) to the glass. Stir for about 30 seconds, or until the mixture is well-chilled.

Place 1 large ice cube in a rocks glass. Strain the mezcal mixture over the ice cube. Garnish the rocks glass with an orange half-wheel. Serve immediately.

ADVICE FROM ALIS

If you're hunting for activated charcoal, you might spot it in the supplement aisle of the grocery store or find it online with a click of your finger. It's the potion that turns your cocktails as dark as the deepest night sky, adding a touch of mystery to your mixology game.

Bloody
Amren

Unleash your inner immortal with this take on a Bloody Mary, a concoction as fierce as Velaris's own second-in-command. Crafted for those who, like Amren, crave the bold and the beautiful (but maybe not the blood), this drink packs a punch with its spiced tomato base. Whether you're deciphering ancient texts or plotting to save Prythian, this drink is your perfect accomplice, offering a sip of sustenance that's almost as invigorating as Amren's favored, more . . . iron-rich, let's say, elixirs. Don't hoard this treasure—it's best shared among friends, or at least with those brave enough to steal a sip from a creature as formidable as Amren.

1 tablespoon kosher salt

¼ teaspoon cayenne pepper

1 slice lemon

Ice

1¼ cups vegetable juice (such as V8)

1½ ounces vodka

½ ounce fresh lemon juice

½ ounce fresh lime juice

¼ ounce balsamic vinegar

¾ teaspoon Madras curry powder

¼ teaspoon sea salt (or more, to taste)

⅛ teaspoon freshly ground black pepper

1 cinnamon stick, for garnish

1 stalk celery, for garnish

On a small plate, combine the kosher salt and cayenne pepper. Cut a slit in the center of the lemon wedge and rub it around the rim of a pint glass. Dip the rim of the glass into the seasoned salt to coat it. Fill the glass with ice and set aside.

In a cocktail shaker filled with ice, combine the vegetable juice, vodka, lemon juice, lime juice, balsamic vinegar, curry powder, salt, and pepper. Shake vigorously until the outside of the shaker becomes frosted, about 30 seconds. Strain the mixture into the prepared glass.

Garnish the glass with a cinnamon stick and a stalk of celery. Serve immediately.

Morrigan's
Sparkle and Spice Punch

Conjure up the sparkling spirit of Mor with this punch, a cocktail that's as vivacious as she is. Inspired by what Feyre describes as her "citrus and cinnamon scent," this punch combines the zestiness of oranges with a hint of warm cinnamon, capturing her essence in every sip. Just like Mor's ability to light up a room and keep even the mightiest on their toes, this punch is perfect for those moments when you want to add a little fun to your gathering.

FOR THE ORANGE REDUCTION

Zest strips from 2 navel oranges

2 cups fresh orange juice (from about 4 navel oranges)

¼ cup sugar

2 cinnamon sticks

One bottle (750 ml) chilled Prosecco or your favorite sparkling white wine

¼ cup triple sec

¼ cup spiced rum

Ice, for serving

Orange slices, for garnish

To make the orange reduction, in a saucepan, combine the orange zest strips, orange juice, sugar, and cinnamon sticks. Set over medium-high heat and bring to a boil. Reduce the heat to medium-low and simmer, stirring occasionally, until the mixture has reduced to 1 cup, about 10 minutes. Strain the mixture through a fine-mesh sieve (or simply remove the cinnamon sticks and orange zest strips) and allow it to cool to room temperature.

In a large pitcher or punch bowl, combine the Prosecco, orange reduction, triple sec, and spiced rum. (If not serving immediately, omit the Prosecco and chill the mixture until you are ready to serve. Add the Prosecco just before serving.)

To serve, fill a stemless wineglass halfway with ice and an orange slice, then ladle or pour the punch over the top.

THE GENTLE GARDENER'S
TOAST

Raise a glass to Elain with this elixir, where every bubbly sip whispers tales of gardens lush and secrets hushed. Inspired by a French 75, but kissed with lavender as a tribute to the sweetest of the Archeron sisters and her green thumb, it's perfect for those who, like Elain, find joy in the blooms. Crafted with a blend of crisp gin, zesty lemon, and homemade lavender syrup and topped with a splash of sparkling wine, this cocktail dazzles with its floral notes and effervescent charm. So, let's toast to the sister who proves that even the gentlest spirits can stir the wildest adventures.

FOR THE LAVENDER SIMPLE SYRUP

½ cup water

½ cup sugar

2 tablespoons dried lavender buds

Ice

1½ ounces gin

½ ounce fresh lemon juice

3 ounces cold sparkling white wine (such as Champagne or Prosecco)

Lemon twist, for garnish

To make the simple syrup, in a small saucepan, combine the water, sugar, and lavender buds over medium heat. Bring the mixture to a simmer, then reduce the heat to low and simmer until the sugar has completely dissolved, 2 to 3 minutes. Remove the saucepan from the heat and allow the syrup to cool completely.

Strain the syrup through a fine-mesh sieve to remove the lavender buds and transfer the syrup to a jar for storage.

Fill a cocktail shaker with ice. Add the gin, lemon juice, and ½ ounce lavender simple syrup (reserve the remaining syrup for another use). Shake the mixture until well-chilled, then strain into a champagne flute. Top with the sparkling wine.

Garnish the glass with a lemon twist. Serve immediately.

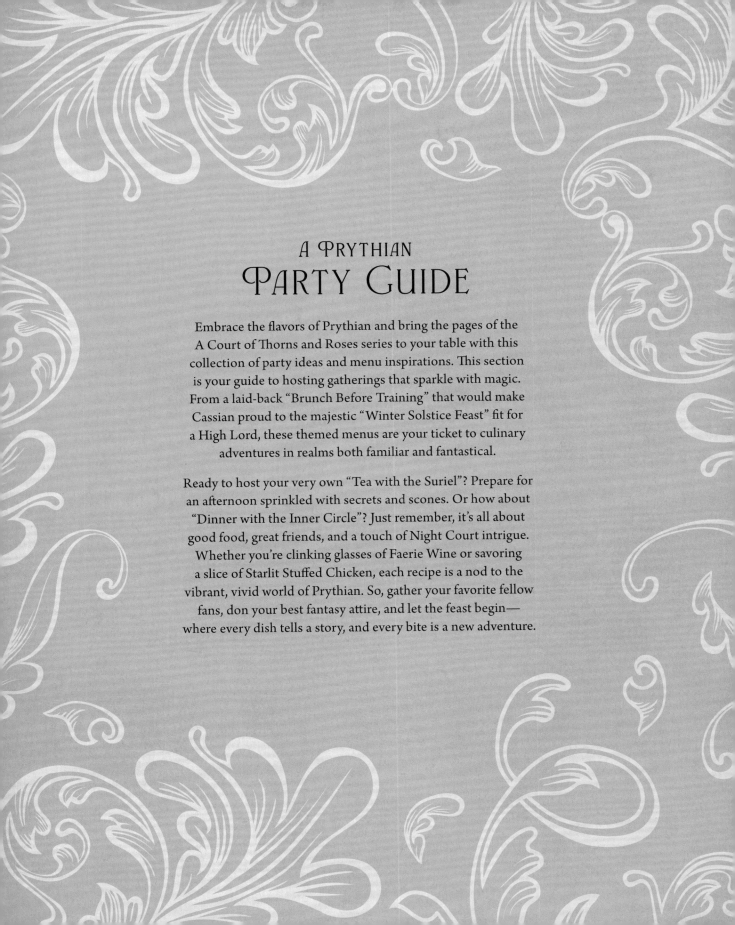

A Prythian
Party Guide

Embrace the flavors of Prythian and bring the pages of the
A Court of Thorns and Roses series to your table with this
collection of party ideas and menu inspirations. This section
is your guide to hosting gatherings that sparkle with magic.
From a laid-back "Brunch Before Training" that would make
Cassian proud to the majestic "Winter Solstice Feast" fit for
a High Lord, these themed menus are your ticket to culinary
adventures in realms both familiar and fantastical.

Ready to host your very own "Tea with the Suriel"? Prepare for
an afternoon sprinkled with secrets and scones. Or how about
"Dinner with the Inner Circle"? Just remember, it's all about
good food, great friends, and a touch of Night Court intrigue.
Whether you're clinking glasses of Faerie Wine or savoring
a slice of Starlit Stuffed Chicken, each recipe is a nod to the
vibrant, vivid world of Prythian. So, gather your favorite fellow
fans, don your best fantasy attire, and let the feast begin—
where every dish tells a story, and every bite is a new adventure.

A COURSE FOR EVERY COURT

Embark on a culinary journey through Prythian with "A Course for Every Court," a potluck-style party where each dish celebrates one of the seven courts. This meal invites you and your friends to bring a piece of Sarah J. Maas's world to your table, with each course a nod to the essence of each court.

For an added bit of fun, invite each guest to represent the court they're bringing a dish for, dressing in colors or styles inspired by their chosen court.

THE MANY FACES OF FEYRE

Step into Feyre Archeron's shoes (or boots) with a Feyre-themed party. It's the perfect excuse to dress up as your favorite iteration of our beloved heroine and bond over some fabulous food. Whether you're all about the full costume experience or just want to focus on the feast, this party is about enjoying the journey of Feyre in the most delicious way possible.

Test your knowledge with a Feyre-themed trivia game—may the biggest fan win. This isn't just any get-together; it's a celebration of Feyre's journey, her ups and downs, and all the magical moments in between. So, come on over, grab a plate, and let's dive into a night of fun, food, and all things Feyre!

SOLSTICE REVELER
Faerie Wine
139

CURSE BREAKER
Wyrm's End Jalapeño Poppers
40

SPRING COURT BRIDE
Simple Lemony Green Salad
30

HUMAN
Merchant's Spiced Chicken Pie
61

DEFENDER OF THE RAINBOW
Artist's Palette Vegetable Gratin
68

HIGH LADY
Jasmine and Blackberry Panna Cotta
99

DINNER with the INNER CIRCLE

Gather your own inner circle for a night inspired by Feyre's memorable first meal with Rhys and the gang at the Night Court. Embrace the camaraderie by serving the meal family-style, just as Feyre experienced.

For an added touch of Night Court magic, engage your guests in a "Secrets of the Court" game. Each guest writes down a trivia question about the Night Court. Throughout the evening, draw these questions at random and have everyone write down the answer. Those who don't answer the question correctly have to drink a good glug of wine (or water, depending on how the night is going!).

Townhouse Slow-Roasted Chicken with Sage and Lemon
64

Simple Lemony Green Salad
30

Sopping Up Crusty Bread
85

Caramel Drizzled Apple Hand Pies
126

To drink, ask each guest to bring a bottle of wine.

Winter Solstice Feast

Celebrate the magic of the Winter Solstice, one of Prythian's most revered festivities, with a grand "Winter Solstice Feast." This feast is designed to mirror the splendor of the longest night of the year as described in the books. Encourage your guests to embrace the occasion with more formal attire, setting the tone for an evening that's both elegant and a grand ol' time. In honor of Feyre's birthday, which happens to fall on this festive night, birthday cupcakes will be served for dessert. And, of course, what feast would be complete without Faerie Wine?

As part of the Winter Solstice Feast, we've got a game for you: "Solstice Story Toasts." This game involves each guest concocting a short, silly prompt for a toast that a character from the series might give. The prompts might be something like "Feyre invited the Suriel to the feast and is thanking it for coming" or "Cassian baked Feyre's birthday cupcakes and is excusing their appearance before they're served."

Upside-Down Onion Parmesan Tarts	Honey and Thyme Caramelized Carrots
33	88
Rosemary and Garlic Roast Beef	Feyre's Birthday Cupcakes
67	129
Cheesy Chive Mashed Potatoes	Faerie Wine
95	139

GAMEPLAY

As guests arrive, have each one write down a random, funny toast prompt related to the Winter Solstice or the ACOTAR series on slips of paper. These could be characters in unusual situations, quirky magical mishaps, or whatever comes to mind. Place these slips into a bowl and mix them up.

At the beginning of the meal, have each guest draw a slip. They can give their toasts as they are called to throughout the meal.

Optional: Have everyone vote for the best toast and have a prize ready for the winner!

SLEEPOVER at the HOUSE

Get ready to kick back and let the magic unfold with a sleepover at The House, just like the cozy night-in that Nesta, Gwyn, and Emerie had in *A Court of Silver Flames*. This is the perfect excuse to gather your besties for an evening filled with laughter, heart-to-heart chats, and great food. Transform your space into your own version of the magical house, complete with comfy cushions, twinkling lights, and your favorite books.

Don't forget the main event: bracelet-making! Dive into a colorful array of threads and charms to create friendship bracelets, pouring your wishes and stories into every twist and turn.

The House's Hearty Pork and Bean Stew
79

Sopping Up Crusty Bread
85

Pistachio Mini Cakes with Whipped Cream and Raspberry Drizzle
132

Cassian's Banned Chocolate Cupcakes
134

Salty Nestas
143

TEA WITH THE SURIEL

Invite your friends to an afternoon of whispered secrets and tasty treats, where intrigue meets indulgence. Inspired by the truth-teller of Prythian, this tea party is a chance to exchange tales as softly as the rustle of leaves in the forests where the Suriel dwells. You'll love every dish on this menu, from the savory Cheese and Chive Scones to the sweet Pistachio Mini Cakes with Whipped Cream and Raspberry Drizzle.

To get the secret sharing going, we're skipping the raw chicken and providing you with a Suriel-inspired game instead, called Secrets and Scones.

In addition to a big pot of tea, of course, here are the recipes you'll need for your tea party:

The Suriel's Almond Tea Cakes
20

Cheese and Chive Scones
22

Wall Watch Chicken Caprese Sandwiches
49

Minty Salad with Brown Butter and Spiced Honey Vinaigrette
34

Pistachio Mini Cakes with Whipped Cream and Raspberry Drizzle
132

GAMEPLAY

As guests arrive, invite them to write down a secret, a little-known fact about themselves, or a harmless confession on a piece of parchment. Keep them light-hearted. Fold the papers and place them in a box or bowl.

Once everyone has settled with their tea and a plate of treats, pass the box around. Each guest takes a turn drawing a piece of paper and reads a secret aloud. The other guests write down who they think wrote that secret.

Once everyone has written their guesses down, the secret sharer reveals themselves. Everyone who guessed correctly gets a point. Repeat until all the secrets are gone.

The winner of the game is the person with the most points! Consider having a small, themed prize for the winner, like a candle in a teacup or a thrifted tea set.

BRUNCH BEFORE TRAINING

Channel the playful and energetic spirit of Cassian before a day of hard work with brunch. This brunch is all about fueling up with tasty, hearty fare with your friends–no actual exertion required (unless you count lifting a fork as a workout).

On the menu are dishes perfect for a leisurely morning, and for a cheeky nod to the formidable Amren, who prefers her meals in a glass, serve up Bloody Amrens, a fiery twist on the classic Bloody Mary–the perfect sipping companion for those who'd rather observe the training than partake in it.

After brunch, maybe opt for a leisurely walk through a park and just leave the training to the Illyrian warriors.

Quiche with Gouda, Bacon, and Leeks
19

Baked Apple Porridge with Spiced Pecans
16

Blueberry-Lemon Cornmeal Muffins
23

Melon Caprese with Lemon Basil Vinaigrette
28

Bloody Amren
146

Acknowledgments

This book is dedicated to my son, Reggie. The idea for this cookbook struck me like a freight train when I was pregnant with him. I emailed a friend who happened to be a literary agent to see if she thought this idea had legs. In what felt like the blink of an eye, I was signing a book deal, eight months pregnant with my first baby and facing a manuscript deadline when he'd be just six months old. I've done hard things before, but the prospect of writing an entire cookbook while navigating new motherhood was nothing short of daunting. The process wasn't easy. (Reggie, remember when you decided independent naps weren't for you, just two weeks out from my deadline? I guess you just knew I needed more cuddles.) But I can't imagine anything better than taking a break from recipe development to play with my baby. This career has allowed me to be home with my son, and since having him, I can't imagine anything more important. He is the greatest thing I've ever done and the biggest source of joy I've ever known. I love you, Reggie.

On that note, thank you to my husband, Eric. You've never ceased to have faith in me and my ideas. You supported me through countless meltdowns—can you imagine the whirlwind of postpartum hormones and looming deadlines? I'm so grateful for your patience, support, and encouragement. I love you, Eric.

To my mom, Laurie: This book (and my sanity) wouldn't exist without the countless hours you spent with Reg so I could focus on work. Thank you for loving me and your grandson so well. Thank you for always being a sounding board for my recipe ideas and for reading *A Court of Thorns and Roses* to better support me while I created this cookbook. We are so lucky to have you. I love you, Mom.

My literary agent, Sally Ekus, is truly the best. Thank you, Sally, for responding so quickly and positively to this idea and for navigating my first book deal. I'm so grateful for your experience, passion, and patience throughout this process. Thank you for fielding my many (many!) questions and always being available for a quick call. You've made this journey so smooth.

Thank you to Edward, my editor, for believing in this project, and for helping me bring this world to life in cookbook form. Working with you has been such a wonderful experience.

Thank you to Amy, Jenn, Lauren F., Lauren L., Kayla, Amelia, and to so many others who let me bounce ideas off you as I worked on this book. This cookbook wouldn't be what it is without your input!

Thank you to friends and family for always being willing guinea pigs and testers yourselves as I worked through recipe after recipe, providing thoughtful feedback. These recipes are all the better for it!

INDEX

Author Bio

Chelsea Cole is a cookbook author and food blogger from Portland, Oregon. Her culinary journey began with her blog, A Duck's Oven, a project started during her time as a student at the University of Oregon. Initially focused on helping students navigate the kitchen, Chelsea's passion for cooking has since expanded to embrace a broader audience, with a particular emphasis on sous vide and pop culture. Chelsea has authored two sous vide cookbooks, *Everyday Sous Vide* and *Sous Vide Meal Prep*, showcasing her love of demystifying complex cooking techniques for home cooks. Now embracing her love of millennial pop culture, Chelsea's current work aims to bring the fantastical dishes from the pages of popular series, TV shows, and movies to the tables of fans everywhere.

Alongside her professional pursuits, Chelsea is usually spending time with her son and husband. Whether she's exploring Portland's culinary scene, camping, in the sidelines at a soccer match, or learning how to make cheese, Chelsea is on a mission to inspire others to get in the kitchen and try something new.

weldon**owen**

an imprint of Insight Editions
P.O. Box 3088
San Rafael, CA 94912
www.weldonowen.com

CEO Raoul Goff
SVP Group Publisher Jeff McLaughlin
VP Publisher Roger Shaw
Executive Editor Edward Ash-Milby
Assistant Editor Kayla Belser
Art Director & Designer Megan Sinead Bingham
Production Designer Jean Hwang
VP Manufacturing Alix Nicholaeff
Senior Production Manager Joshua Smith
Strategic Production Planner Lina s Palma-Temena

Weldon Owen would also like to thank Jen Newens for her work on this book.

Illustrations by Jill De Haan

Photography by Waterbury Publications, Inc.

ISBN: 979-8-88674-192-6

Manufactured in China by Insight Editions
10 9 8 7 6 5 4 3 2 1

ROOTS of PEACE   🌿 REPLANTED PAPER

Insight Editions, in association with Roots of Peace, will plant two trees for each tree used in the manufacturing of this book. Roots of Peace is an internationally renowned humanitarian organization dedicated to eradicating land mines worldwide and converting war-torn lands into productive farms and wildlife habitats. Roots of Peace will plant two million fruit and nut trees in Afghanistan and provide farmers there with the skills and support necessary for sustainable land use.